Four-Claws

Four-Claws

by

Paul Chapman

ISBN: 9798416884109
Imprint: Independently published

Dedication

To Chuck, my brother, to all our crazy adventures. A reminder of all the crazy things we saw when were out hunting. To all my Native family, we all know the realness of some of these things. These mountains hold many secrets and unbelievable events.

One

The Eldorado National Forest near Indian Gulch, or what is known as WestPoint, California, is a place full of mystery, beauty, and evil. People disappear in the area near WestPoint regularly, and serial killers are known to work in that area. The Amador and Calaveras areas were the last places for people to have been seen before they came up missing.   The indigenous people tell tales of Skinwalkers or shapeshifters that roam the area. There are even tales of red-headed giants that have been seen in these woods. The Natives have a tale of trapping giants in a cave, setting a fire at the mouth of the cave, and killing them with the smoke. Outsiders say that these are just tales or myths. They may say whatever makes them happy.

Many Native people from the Haplogroup X and Haplogroup X2 have similar tales. The mound builders, pyramid builders, and sky people from the stars all play a part. Some call them watchers, Nephilim, Anunnaki, Angels, Demons, or a cornucopia of names. The storylines always stay the same. It is the story of someone from another planet landing here and interacting with humans.

The trees in the Eldorado are thick and supply plenty of secrecy. The trees absorb the sounds of screams and other noises. The beautiful scenery lends itself to plenty of victims drawn there to enjoy the sights and explore the caves.

The Natives have been in this area since the dawn of time before the Americas. This place has an energy that the Natives knew about long ago. The energy seems to draw evil and magical things to it. The wood of Indian Gulch is a vortex that pulls things towards it. The natives that have lived here in this area tell many tales of horrific and fantastic things.

This place is where Blaine Four-Claws was born into a whirlwind of pain and destruction. The people who were Blaine's adoptive parents were part of a demonic cult that practiced the black arts out in the forest. Several hunters over the years had met their doom because they stumbled across the cult. The cult had many circles of skulls and other bones in the forest. Many times, the circles would be twenty to thirty feet across. Animal skulls surround the circles with an oak tree at the center. Inside the circle of skulls is a pentagram of long bones.

There are darker areas of magic in the wood that even the Natives do not like to visit. These dark magic areas of human skulls and bones were found very deep in the Eldorado. The Eldorado National Forest, Indian Gulch, WestPoint, is the home of Charles Ng and Leonard Lake. Lake and Ng were the serial killer duo that killed 25 people, primarily children and young women. These men brought evil and pain to the WestPoint area. A blemish that would remain for decades.

The deer seemed to avoid the evil circles like it was poison or radioactivity. The lack of birdsong made the evil feel so strong that it felt like you could cut it with a knife. There were always dark splotches of dirt in the middle caused by the dark reddish blood black. Animals avoided this area at all costs. Hell, even the coyote and wolves would not go near it.

Others lived in the area during Lake and Ng that partook of the evil, and the public never heard of them. These were the kin of Blaine that created Blaine Four-Claws. If it were not for Crooked-man, Blaine would be dead. Crooked-man and his brother Two-Coins took the police to the pentagram of human bones and skulls. Crooked-Man broke the rule of silence with the shapeshifters and told the outsiders of the actions the night Blaine was to die. Crooked-man and his brother Two-Coins paid the price for breaking the silence. The consequence is that Crooked-man and Two-Coins will forever walk the roads of Indian Gulch for their breach of silence. You can still find them today, walking backward down the roads leading into Indian Gulch. You will see them ten miles out of town. When you get into the town, they will be sitting on the bench in front of the bar. Crooked-man and Two-coins spirits are forever in the in-between. Visitors do not know and do not understand the ways of the Native people, so no one bothers to tell the visitors the truth. I tell you now, and you still do not believe, even though it has been written and told for thousands of years. You still believe it is a fairy-tale, a myth made up by ignorant people. You cannot explain how things were built, even though we tell you.

Like your Constitution, our people had the Five Nations Iroquois Confederacy, which is hundreds of years older-1142. However, people still believed we were ignorant savages, even though we had farms and a government.

Your truth; is not my truth. My reality; does not coincide with your science. Your history; is not my history. Your beliefs do not change what happens here in these woods. Your gods have no power in these woods. Natives have written these tales; we have kept these stories alive to pass down and keep the knowledge alive. The evil we warned you about has always been here waiting. We did not bring evil.

We often wonder why you mock us for our ways and our beliefs. You do not believe your own tales in your religious book, and that book talks of the giants and the sky people. You have the answers to the universe and do not see them. You cannot even believe in your own Elijah that was taken into the heavens by a craft. Funny how you believe what you want and ignore the rest. Who are you to call us ignorant savages?

Two

Blaine woke up with a start. His heart was racing, and he was hot as fire. He closed his eyes and could see the man dying. The man's blood steamed as it flowed out along the pavement. Blaine watched him as the light went out in his eyes. He could feel the stickiness of the blood on his own hands as if he held the knife that slit the man's throat. Blaine looked in the window of a building, and he saw himself standing there with a knife in his hands.

These dreams were dark magic, which was not right, and he had been having these dreams or visions for several weeks now. He felt like he needed to tell someone, but whom. No one listened to him when he talked about his dreams, and his adopted parents did not listen, and it made them uncomfortable.

Blaine was aware of his past and how it made his adoptive parents feel. Blaine had never asked to see any of his fellow tribal members or family. He had never even driven the ninety miles from Modesto to WestPoint to try and find any family he might have on the local reservations. That history was closed for him, and Blaine did not want to change that fact. He had heard stories about it, and that was good enough.

Blaine was scared. He did not know what to do about the dreams. They were very vivid. The dreams were not like anything he had ever experienced. He had "feelings" about things at times. The "feelings" always turned out to be true. It made everyone avoid him, so he stopped telling people about them. Blaine knew they were real and that he had a gift. Now. Well, now he had these damn dreams. What if these were real? What should he do?

He looked at the clock and groaned. He was going to be late for class at Modesto Junior College or MJC. He grabbed a baseball cap and took off out the door. He got in his 1972 VW bug, "Teddy." It used to be a beige color until he got tired of being teased that he was driving a serial killer car. Blaine painted it with a spray can of gray primer to not look like a Ted Bundy car.

The car rumbled to life. Blaine took off down the street with a cloud of bluish smoke following him. He could barely see his house in the mirror because of all the smoke. Blaine knew he had to rebuild the engine soon.

Biology class was on the right side of campus towards the front. Blaine hated that it started so early in the morning. He went into the cafeteria to get an energy drink. As he readied to pay, he saw the newspaper. The headline said that a man had been murdered. He bought the paper so he could read what had happened. He wondered if it was the same man.

The paper did not help much. The article reported that the man was attacked by the bus terminal on 9th street. Folding the newspaper, he shoved it into his backpack and ran to class.

He thought about the dream so much that he did not pay attention in class. He missed the notes on the board that warned of a test on Thursday. Blaine's week was about to get much worse.

There was a ticket on the window of Teddy. Blaine had thought he could get away with parking in the staff area. He got caught and now would have to pay $25! He did not have an extra $25 bucks. He slammed the door to the car and headed home. He had to mow the yard and do the laundry. His parents did not mind him going to college and not working if he did work around the house.

The radio droned on with useless advertisements and a news flash about the murdered man. A suspect had been apprehended, and it turns out it was the homeless man's drinking buddy.

Blaine felt instantly better. For some reason, he felt like he was absolved of some sort of guilt. He felt like he would sleep better tonight. He could not stop asking himself why it was his image he saw in the window in his dream, and he could not shake the idea that there was something to it.

Blaine took a shower after his chores and laid down to take a nap. As he lay there sleeping, he was overcome by the dream again. This time he could see the face of the killer in the window, and it was not his image but that of a scruffy white-haired man with a bright blue jacket. Blaine woke up from his nap and started dinner for his parents.

At times Blaine felt like a servant at his house. It was not just the chores that he did, but he seemed disconnected from his parents. He tried hard to be warmer towards them. However, they were also very cold and distant people with few friends. They did not talk much like spouses and talked even less to Blaine. His life had always seemed to be a solitary existence. Blaine often wondered if it was his own past or personality that caused them to behave that way toward him. He knew deep in his heart that they loved him after all, who would save a broken and damaged Native boy from such an evil place that involved such an evil event.

Blaine turned on the nightly news KCRA 3 to watch while he cooked. He was cooking his dad's favorite, fettuccine alfredo, with Italian sausage. Blaine was boiling the water for the noodles when the news about the murder in Modesto was broadcasted. The image of the man in the light blue coat seemed to stare at Blaine from the television screen. He looked just like he did in Blaine's dream.

The water boiled over the side of the pot. Foamy water poured out over the stove and the floor as Blaine stood there with his mouth hanging open. The reporter changed the story. Blaine noticed the mess he created while staring blankly at the television. He took a roll of paper towels out of the cabinet and started cleaning up the mess. Blaine was still shaky when his parents got home.

They ate a quiet dinner and then watched Family Feud. There was very little conversation between anyone, and then they all went off to bed. At the top of the stairs, Blaine's parents went right to their room, and Blaine went to the left to his room.

Blaine's room was at the very end of the hall on the house's long side. It was a four-bedroom house with one master bedroom downstairs, a master bedroom upstairs, and two other bedrooms upstairs. There were four bathrooms, two downstairs and two upstairs. It was a very nice 3,500 square foot home with a large backyard and a big pool with a pool house with a bedroom, bathroom, and kitchen. There was a four-car garage and large metal shop at the very back of the two-acre property. The house was on the outskirts of Modesto on the edge of town and country. The property afforded Blaine's father, Rick, to work on his hotrods in the shop at the back of the property. Blaine's mother was a middle-school math teacher that knitted for her hobby. She had hundreds of knitted blankets around the house. Each room had a knitted comforter on the beds. Downstairs had a library at the far end of the house with a large comfortable leather couch. Blaine would fall asleep on that couch often while reading for classes. A large bay window looked out onto the backyard pool area. The pool house was out of the view to the room's left. It was a beautiful home full of warm tile floors and a rich mahogany wood staircase, shelves, and furniture.

Blaine closed his door softly behind him. He stood thinking about going downstairs to read for a while to help him fall asleep. He let out a sigh, and instead, he lay down on his bed and stared at the ceiling until he fell into a restless sleep.

His dreams were brutal tonight. He had not had dreams like these in a
very long time. He could not wake up, and he broke out into a hot,
sweaty nightmare.

Three

In the mid-1980s, Carl Broad Knife Johnson (Osiris he called himself) and his wife, Trisha Johnson, lived in WestPoint, California. Carl met Charles Ng and Leonard Lake at the gas station in WestPoint. That chatted about the locals a little bit. They ended up forming a strange relationship that would cause many to suffer. You see, Carl had been reading many books about the dark arts, Satanism, and Grimoires. It was that kind of stuff that interested Leonard. A few months later, Carl had started to create large clearings that he would encircle with goat skulls, deer skulls, and other animal skulls. Carl would collect the roadkill and clean and bleach the skulls to add to his circles. Carl would then take the long bones that he had collected and create a pentagram in the middle of the circles. Over a year or so, he had created three of these circles. Carl would hold his Satanic ceremonies that he read about in the middle of these circles. The word got around, and some of the Natives that Carl grew up with started hanging out with him.

As time grew and he became closer to Ng and Lake, Carl was given some human bones, which set things into high gear. Carl created a circle using human skulls. The circle started with three skulls and eventually ended with ten human skulls. These skulls came from the many victims of Ng and Lake and a couple of hunters that trespassed into the sacred circle of Carl Broad Knife.

The leg bones Carl used for the pentagram were a mix of human and animal bones. Carl had not killed enough people to supply enough bones to finish the forty-foot wide circle. An old oak tree stood at the circle's center with a large granite boulder with a flat top that sloped down slightly on one end. Carl began calling himself Osirus because he read about an Egyptian high priest with that name, so he thought he would use the name to incite mystery.

Osirus began to conduct black magic rituals and Satanic rituals at the circle with the human skulls. It did not take long to gain some followers of like-minded ideas. Many were tweakers (meth addicts) that had consumed so many drugs that their brains were fried, and they had become schizophrenic. This was a ready-made cult that seemed to be looking for a leader, and Osirus was that leader.

The beginning of the end for this group happened in September during deer season. Two hunters, Jim and Chuck, stumbled upon the circle by accident. Some cult members were camped out in the woods near the rocks, and they spotted the hunters and kept a close watch on them. The circle was still two-hundred yards into the forest.

Jim and Chuck followed the valley in a northerly direction. The sun began to peek over the mountain range to their right-hand side. Their hot breath came out in plumes of smoke. Jim started towards the right side as it began to rise. Chuck followed the flat valley floor, rising towards the ridge. The edge of the valley had an outcropping of rock covered in pines. Chuck walked towards the outcropping. He climbed up onto the outcropping and came into an opening. He walked towards the oak tree and stopped to take a piss. He leaned his rifle against the big rock next to the tree and relieved himself. As he was urinating, he looked around and noticed the oddness of the circle he was standing in.

"Hey! Jim, come and look at this shit."

Jim trudged over towards Chuck's direction, "Where are you, dumbass?"

"Up the draw, on top of these rocks. Jesus, Jim, this shit is crazy."

Jim kicks what he thought was a large stone and looks down to his horror at a human skull. "Hey Chuck, look at this shit. What the fuck?"

"What do you see?"

"Chuck, there is a human skull over here. What the fuck."

"Wait. What? No way, Jim, there is a rock with blood on it over here."

The two men are freaking out as they begin to really look at the circle. The evil of the place begins to wash over them.

"Chuck! We need to get out of here. Now"

"I agree, Jim. Let's get the fuck outta here."

Jim and Chuck began to make their way out of the area, they heard a noise off to their left. Something is following them. The men begin to get scared and pick up their pace. Jim takes his rifle off his shoulder and carries it like he did in Vietnam. Chuck copies what Jim does, and they keep their head on a swivel. After two hundred yards of travel, the men calm down. They begin to joke about what just happened.

When they get to camp, Jim jokes with Chuck about pissing on the tree in the middle of the weird circle. They laugh about it and begin to fix some breakfast. Their hunting is over for the morning. They will go out again around four. They will hunt until dusk.

The campground was empty during the week. Jim and Chuck were all by themselves, and they liked it that way. It was a relief to get away from their old ladies and home. The two got into the truck and drove up highway four to Alpine Lake to fish. When they got back, they would go out hunting again.

As the two men drove off through the campground, three figures stood in the woods, watching them go. They knew where the camp was, and they knew what their truck looked like. The three figures walked into the deserted camp. One of the figures adds something to the coffee pot on the edge of the fire pit. The pot was full, so the men would warm it back up and not pour it out. The three figures went back into the woods. One of them would stay and wait for the men to come back. The other two would go and tell Osirus what had happened.

Osirus listened to the story about what had happened that morning. He was angry at the man that had urinated in the sacred circle. Osirus would make him pay dearly for that transgression. The other man would be killed, but the man who pissed in the circle would pray for death.

The two men that brought the information were sent back to wait for the men to come back. Then they would bring them back alive to Osirus. They took the old brown Chevy pickup. It had an old beat-up camper shell on the bed.

Four

The locals can tell you about Crooked-man and Two-coins. Most people have their stories about the two men they see on the side of the road. Crooked-man walks on the right-side of the road backward-facing traffic, and Two-coins walks on the left-side of the road backward-facing traffic. People talk about seeing these two men ten or twenty miles out of town, but when they arrive in town, the two are there at the gas station or in front of the bar. People are baffled at the two. Many just think that it is several Indians that walk that way. The Tribe knows who and what they are. They know their abilities, and they leave them alone. They are shapeshifters; some say skin-walkers.

Crooked-Man started walking backward down the road because he was hit by a pickup while walking these roads. Pretty simple if you think about it. Two-coins walked that way because his older brother walked that way. There is no mystery in that. However, their abilities to be seen ten or twenty miles from town and then end up in town before you could drive that distance? That was as real as the road you drive on. These old men had a special gift that was not of this world. So, when the Natives tell you of a coyote walking on its hindlegs? It is likely Crooked-man and his brother Two-coins; they are shapeshifters. They are as real as the road you drive on. Many times, death follows in the wake of these men. They have gifts and curses that others do not understand. They see things we do not see.

It was Crooked-Man that Jim and Chuck saw driving back from Alpine lake. They did not see Two-coins on the other side of the road. Jim and Chuck were going into WestPoint or Indian Gulch to lunch from 88 Burger in Pioneer. Ten miles between Alpine and WestPoint, Jim and Chuck passed Crooked-man and Two-coins walking on the road.

"Hey, Jim, did you see those two?"

"They can't be the same men, Chuckles. It must be some other Indians. They are weird as shit up here."

The two kept talking about the weird shit they had seen that day. They still had about ten more miles to get into WestPoint. Two deer crossed the road ahead of them. They pulled over and followed the deer into the woods. The deer went off to the left, and Jim and Chuck started to go straight towards a flat area ahead. Chuck looked down and saw a goat skull. Jim gasped as he looked around at stick figures hanging in the trees.

It was another circle made from bones. The men turned around and left without a word. As they came out of the woods, Crooked-man and Two-coins were standing leaning against the truck bed, watching Jim and Chuck as they walked towards them with their guns in their hands at the ready.

Crooked-Man spoke first, "You city boys would do with some caution. These woods are not for you."

Two-coins spoke after his brother, "Not good woods for people at all. No good for anyone. The animals don't even like it here."

"We agree with you," Jim agreed with the men.

"Um yeah," Chuck agreed, "No disrespect, but this place is weird as shit."

Crooked-man cleared his throat, "There is evil in these woods now. Not all skins are evil, but there are others as well. They bring evil here. It is not safe. You should go home."

With that, Crooked-man and Two-coins walked into the woods opposite of the side with the circle of bones.

Jim and Chuck got in the truck and headed towards Pioneer. As they came up to the town of WestPoint, they spotted Crooked-man and Two-coins sitting in front of the bar.

"No fucking way!" Jim pointed.

"Holy shit, Jim, no one will believe that shit if we told them."

When the two got to Pioneer and ordered their burgers, they talked to the locals. They asked if they had ever seen two old Native American guys walking on the road backward. All the locals chimed in, "Let me guess, you passed them up ten miles back on the road, and they beat you into town?"

Jim was confused, "Yeah, how did you know. Is that shit real?"

"Oh yes, that is Crooked-man and Two-coins. They are elders in the Tribe, and everyone knows them," Sue turns to turn the burgers on the grill.

"Yeah," Chuck chimes in, "the old guy that is all hunched over told us to get out of these woods and go home."

The man at the end of the counter gets up, "Why? Why should Crooked-Man talk to you? What did you do?"

"We found some weird circle in the forest on the side of the road. That Crooked guy and his buddy were standing at our truck when we came out of the woods," Chuck swallowed hard. "They told us to go home."

"You walked into the circle, didn't you? Crooked-Man never talks to anyone, and bad things happen to those he talks to." The man at the end of the counter stared at them.

"Chuck pissed in one of these circles on accident," Jim laughed.

The man at the end of the counter abruptly left the burger stand. Sue stood looking at the men with her mouth open. She walked over and picked up a shell in it was a bundle and a feather in it. She lit the bundle with a lighter and began spreading the smoke with a feather chanting something. It was a sickly-sweet smell.

"What the fuck is that shit?" Chuck blurted out.

Jim crinkled up his nose, bagged up their burgers, "You folks are weird as shit."

"Go, Home," Sue yelled at them as they walked out shaking.

Jim and Chuck got in their truck and drove back to camp. The two old Indians were not in WestPoint when they drove through, and Jim and Chuck did not even talk on their way back to the camp.

The sun was up overhead when they got back into camp. It was two in the afternoon. Without saying much, the two men began to pack up their camp. Jim poured some coffee in two cups and added some Jameson whiskey. The two men stood looking at the campfire, and they were stunned into silence. Jim poured the rest of the coffee into the smoldering fire. The tent was secured into the bed of the truck. The guns were unloaded and, in their cases, in the back of the four-door diesel F450 dually.

Chuck sat down on a picnic bench at the campsite. He was suddenly very tired, and he wanted to go home and get out of these weird-ass woods.

Jim sat in the front seat of the truck with the engine running. He leaned against the steering wheel and fell asleep. The truck rumbled as the figures in the old brown Chevy watched and waited.

Crooked-man and Two-coins stood on a bluff above the campground and watched. It was too late for these city boys, and they had tried to warn them. They came down from their hindlegs onto all fours and slowly ran off into the forest. Nightfall would be here soon.

Five

Jim awoke first. He shook his head violently, trying to clear the cobwebs in his head. It was pitch black outside and bitterly cold. He could smell smoke and see the glow of a fire. He tried to move, and he could not move. He was tied to the side of the big Oaktree. Chuck lay on the big flat rock beside it.

Jim's mouth ached. He realized that something was wrong with his tongue. It was gone, and he could not feel it. His lips felt sticky and crusty. His chin felt wet. He tried hard to yell but could only manage a muffled groan. He had a rag stuffed into his mouth. He fought hard against the ropes. He could hear laughing and snickering in the dark.

Chuck began to wake up. He tried to sit up. He could not because his arms and legs were tied to stakes on the four corners of the rock. He was on his back. He screams a loud scream that rang out into the darkness. Two coyotes sat in the dark woods watching. Carl Broad Knife was Native, and he had gone a dark road. Crooked-man and Two-coins watched in sadness. They did not care about the white men. They only cared about their own and the evil they were indulging in. The evil had spread from the ones called Leonard Lake and Charles Ng. The evil had infected many people in these woods.

Osirus walked into the light of the fire in his white robe, dark red shirt, and deer hide breeches. He held an old flint knife with an antler handle in his hand. As he walked by the man on the rock, he sliced the sole of the man's foot. The man screamed loudly. No one outside of this circle would hear this poor man. The man tied to the tree moaned, and the man tied to the rock looked at him with wide, scared eyes running with tears. Osirus walked behind the man tied to the tree, and he reached around the tree and cut the man's throat.

Jim felt a stinging sensation across his throat and was surprised. This could not be happening. It was all a dream. The front of his belly and pants were hot and wet. Chuck watched Jim and screamed. He fought against his ropes as Jim bled out. Jim simply went to sleep. He did not feel much pain or even fully understand what was happening. He just simply died. His family would never know what happened to the two men. They went hunting and just disappeared. That would be all there was to them—just missing people among thousands of missing people.

Osirus walked towards the man on the rock. The man screamed and cried out for his cousin Jim. Osirus cut the Achilles tendon on both legs and then cut the tendons behind the knees and across the kneecaps. He watched as the man flailed his thighs up and down, trying to get his lower limbs to work. Osirus cut into the tendons of the biceps in the ditch of each arm. Osirus methodically cut all the tendons in the shoulders, making the arms useless. Osirus walked away from the man on the rock.

Chuck's voice was harsh and had more of a croaking sound than screaming. Hours had passed since this had all begun. He was feeling dizzy and had vomited on himself several times. Tears wet his eyes. He stared wildly around him, looking for the man that was torturing him. Chuck saw the man approach him with a book in his hand, chanting some words. He saw the man walk towards him, and someone gave the man a white-hot fire poker. The man plunged the poker into Chuck's right eye. Chuck began to scream, but his chest cramped up. The cramp hurt so bad. Dark spots danced in front of Chuck as he died of a heart attack. He lay still on the rock.

Osirus continued to poke at the other eye, and the body lay still. The burnt flesh smell permeated the whole circle. The thick smell of blood, vomit, and excrement filled the night. Osirus cursed when he finally figured out that the man on the rock was dead.

The other cult members put out the fire and left the bodies tied up. Everyone went to their beds and fell fast asleep. They would clean up and prepare the bodies to collect the bones and bleach them. The bones would stay and become part of the circle.

The two coyotes watched as the cult members and Carl Broad Knife left. They watched the bodies for hours in the dark of night. They were sad for Carl Broadknife because he had been polluted by evil.

Crooked-man and Two-coins traveled that night over to the house of Lake and Ng. It smelled of death. The two men had killed many people here, and they were still killing. They were evil men, and their evil had corrupted others here. Crooked-Man wondered what to do about it. Should he get involved or leave it be. After all, they were outsiders, but they had brought evil with them. That evil was spreading to the Natives.

Six

Blaine woke up from his nightmare. It was a vision from an elder long ago. Blaine did not want these visions. He did not want to be part of his ancestry, and he wanted to distance himself from them and their ways. He had heard of Crooked-Man and knew who he was. Blaine wished this would stop and go away.

A coyote rose on its hind legs and looked towards the house. He could smell the nightmare that Blaine was having It came down on all fours and ran off into the night.

Blaine rolled over and went back to sleep. His nightmare soon followed, and Blaine's room seemed to drop several degrees. The scent of a campfire crept into the room, and Blaine could hear chanting off in the distance.

He could feel the cold rock by the oak tree in that circle of evil. His older brother, Chaske, meaning the first son, lay beside him. His chosen brother, the firstborn. His father Osirus and his mother stood with the other members of the cult in a ceremony that would bind the two souls of the brothers. The ritual would end up giving Blaine the name Four-claws. Blaine was supposed to be sacrificed, and his blood was to anoint his brother Chaske and bind their souls together.

As the ceremony reached a crescendo and Blaine was to be sacrificed. A bear broke into the circle, followed by two wolves. Chaske had a deep cut across his chest where Blaine was to baptize Chaske with his blood as Blaine died. The bear killed Osirus with one quick swipe of its vast four-clawed paw. The swipe knocked Osirus over the rock with the two boys on it. The paw came down onto Blaine's chest and carved four long furrows clear to the bone. Chaske ended up on top of Blaine. Chaske's body was convulsing in its death throes. It was supposed to be the other way around.

Blaine did not want this. He tossed and turned in his nightmare. The cult members scattered and ran to the four winds. His mother was mauled by the bear and left for dead. The two wolves lay down by the rock protecting Blaine and further harm. Crooked-Man stood up after all the cult members left and pulled Chaske's dead off him and put poultices on the wounds across Blaine's chest. The police were late in showing up as always. Crooked-Man had broken the treaty of silence and brought outsiders in. Crooked-Man and Two-Coins had brought in the elder Three-Bears. They had resolved the evil that had cursed the tribe for too long. They did not want to kill anyone. Bodies of the Carl Broad Knife "Osirus" Johnson lay dead, along with his wife Trisha, a white outsider woman anyway. Several cult members also lay dead from being mauled by wolves, Crooked-man and Two-coins. The first child, Chaske, lay dead on the rock as well. Blaine would be taken to the reservation and cared for until a foster family could adopt him.

When the police arrived all, they managed to do was to clean up. The police had no clue what had happened, so the police documented the circle with the human skulls. Instead of checking to see if any skulls could be identified, they buried them all in a mass grave. The secret remained in WestPoint, and it was never to be spoken about. It has never been spoken of until now. Leonard Lake and Charles Ng would be found out later that year. Because of the interference of Crooked-man and Two-coins, they too paid the price. They are now banished to the land in-between. Forever to walk the same roads in silence as an example to others to keep the silence and not bring in outsiders.

Blaine woke up sweaty and sick. With every nightmare came more information he did not want to know. More questions popped up with every nightmare as well. He could not help to think that this curse was not over yet. Blaine knew that there was more on the horizon. There was evil lurking in the shadows waiting to enter his life and continue its path of destruction. It seemed like Blaine would have to continue to pay the price for what his father did.

Blaine had been told that Crooked-man and Two-coins were his uncles. This made Blaine more confused, and all Blaine wanted was for all of this to end.

Seven

Sam and Roger had been partners in the homicide division of Modesto Police Department for at least a decade. The current homicide victims seemed to be a bit different this time around. The suspect was caught very quickly, but he had no recollection of doing the crime. The video surveillance from the bus terminal supplies proof of who did the murder. The suspect could not believe he had killed his best friend, Carl, and was legitimately upset that he had done the crime after seeing the video.

Sam is fed up with the obvious lie the man had been telling, and he lets the man see the video. The man's reaction was not what Sam and Roger were expecting, and the man was grief-stricken by what he saw—the clear outcome of it all. In Mr. Mackey's voice from South Park, Sam says, "Drugs are bad, m'kay."

Sam has a very dark sense of humor, and Roger has a dark sense of humor when not depressed. You see, Roger is dealing with the death of his wife, and he is a heavy drinker, and it is interfering with his daily life.

"Well, that is another one for the books," Sam checks off the homicide on the board.

Roger laughs, "48-hours, my ass. The people on that show are low and slow." The two men laugh about Roger's joke.

The men feel there is nothing to investigate because it is an open and shut case. Move along people, nothing to see here, folks. It is a typical emotional murder from a couple of drunks.

Sam and Roger go home to get some sleep. They will come back to work tomorrow at 7 am if they are not called out tonight.

Sam lives with his wife of thirty years. High school sweethearts. After Sam and Luan graduated from college at Stanislaus State University, they were married. Luan works as a city manager, and Sam is a detective. A perfect match for big city life. They both make good salaries, and they live in a costly neighborhood. Luan's parents left them twenty acres of land in the housing area known as Del Rio. Her parents helped them build their house when Del Rio was first started. Their home is now worth three to four million because it sits on four acres of land. Luan knew about the development because she works in the city planning office. So, they sold the other 16 acres a little at a time. It was a gold mine for them. They could have retired with the money they received for the property.

Roger, on the other hand. Roger went to Downey High, the local school for the airport district. The neighborhood used to be low-income; the white people there lived a meager life in the airport district of Modesto. Roger always said he was white trash and then laughed about it. He had never gone to a university. He attended Modesto Junior College and received an AS degree in criminal science. He felt he belonged here until all the gangs moved into the area. It was a crime-ridden neighborhood that Roger was called to this neighborhood as a homicide detective regularly. Roger and his wife, Lexy, bought their house many years ago as a starter house. They paid it off quickly. However, they never did anything about trying to invest or move or anything. It was like they were just stuck in time. Then the worst thing happened. Lexy was murdered. It happened in the neighborhood they lived in; It was a senseless murder caused by being in the wrong place at the wrong time. She was getting a pack of smokes at the corner store when a gunfight between rival gangs broke out. She was hit in the head by a random bullet intended for someone else. It didn't matter because she was dead. Roger blamed himself for not trying to move out of the area. He had become complacent. He was like a frog in boiling water. He did not see the danger. Lexy did not see the danger either. None of this logic helped Roger deal with her death. He went to counseling and drank himself to sleep most nights in the same house they lived in for years. Roger would never move now. The house kept Lexy close to him and reminded him of her death every day.

Roger used to like to fish when he was younger. Lexy and Roger had a fourteen-foot Valco aluminum boat with a ten-horse-power motor and a trolling motor. They used to go the river down the street and fish in the Tuolumne River. They could travel five to ten miles upstream to Fox Grove and Fish. Fox Grove was the furthest upstream they could go. The water got very shallow before they got to the Waterford bridge.

The Modesto Airport was five houses away from Roger, and the local elementary school was next door. He and Lexy never did have kids. However, that is why they bought the damn house next to the school. The older people in the neighborhood were great, and the new people brought the gangs and crime.

Roger drank some whiskey and set the glass down next to his .45 ACP Kimber 1911. He pulled the action back and loaded it. He stuck the barrel in his mouth and breathed deep. He took it out and dropped the magazine from the pistol, pulled the slide back, and ejected the shell. This was a daily ritual that Roger did. Take a drink, contemplate suicide. Put his pistol up. Drink until he passes out—every damn day since Lexy died. The gun oil clung to his tongue. The whiskey did not wash it away. The whiskey did not wash anything away. It only put him to sleep until he did it all over tomorrow. One day he would grow some balls and pull the trigger. One day, today was not the day, "Not today, Satan!" Roger laughed at himself. He spits on the floor and takes another drink of whiskey. Roger fills it up and downs the glass of whiskey. He sits back in his recliner and passes out.

Outside, gunshots can be heard in the neighborhood. Cars are racing up and down the street, and Roger is blissfully unaware. He sleeps the rest of an alcoholic, and he is dead to the world.

Eight

Two weeks later, near the Ninth Street bridge there was a murder that took place there over the river. A nude woman was hanging from the trestle over the water with the name, Chaske, carved into the chest. The name of the homeless woman was Trisha. None of this information would make the newspaper because her boyfriend would be charged with the murder. The only reason it was reported was that people driving by on the Ninth Street bridge could see her body hanging from the trestle. The police wrote it off as another drunken brawl among the growing homeless population.

Blaine had not had any dreams at all in the last two weeks. That is until tonight. He did not see the name on the victim's chest and did not know her name. Blaine did not know the name of the first victim. How could he? No one told him. He did dream about her death. He did not know that the police had already caught the murderer. Blaine called the police to tell them about his dream, and what the murderer looked like. Blaine described him perfectly. The dream piqued Sam's interest a little, but not enough to have an interview over it. Sam hung up the phone and forgot about it.

Blaine felt stupid to call. He beat himself up over it all day because he was embarrassed to have said anything. From now on, he would not say anything at all.

Roger and Sam interrogated Trisha's boyfriend. They asked about the letters carved on her chest. What did it mean? Was it some guy's name she was cheating with? Why hang her from the bridge swinging over the water for everyone to see? How did he do it? Why? Why? Why?

Just like the other guy from the first victim, he cried. He and his old lady were just drinking, not fighting. Ask everyone. We never fought.

The witnesses did say that the couple did not fight. They had been together for years. They used to work at a construction company together. When the economy crashed, they got laid off and ended up homeless. They began to drink, and bingo twenty years go by, and Bob's your uncle.

The suspect had no idea how it all happened. The suspect passed out and woke up on the river bank, being shaken awake by the police. The strange thing is that they did not hang out down by the Ninth Street bridge. They were drinking at La Loma Park, miles away from where she died. He had no idea of how they got there. He had her blood all over him and had a knife in his pocket with her blood on it. It was another open and shut case.

They wrapped it all up to drinking and drugs. The district attorney pressed charges, and that was it. The only real weird thing was this Blaine kid that called in the description of Trisha and her killer. How did this kid know that unless he had seen it? Even though he said, he had a dream about it. He did not know their names or even that Trisha had letters carved across her naked chest. So, he did not have all the information. Witnesses from the bridge could tell she had something carved in her even from that distance.

Sam and Roger ignored the phone call from Blaine. Blaine could not understand why he felt the need to call and tell the police what he did tell them. What did he hope to get out of it? They rejected him like everyone else. Life for Blaine was like a broken record of rejection. People want to get rid of Blaine. People were ignoring Blaine. No one wants him. It just replayed over and over. Even with all that BS in his life, he never became depressed; he never wanted to give up and quit. Never one time did he ever contemplate suicide. He was a genuinely happy person. It was this trait and quality that Crooked-Man had seen in Blaine. He knew Blaine was important and had to be saved. It is the reason that Crooked-Man followed Blaine to man to Modesto. He had to watch over him to make sure he was safe and warn him of danger. Two-coins could still be seen in WestPoint walking the roads. Crooked-Man was here in Modesto. The in-between world was buzzing with danger and evil. Death was in the air.

Blaine walked out to the shop to see what his dad was working on. This was the only way to get the man to talk to him. The light from the shop glowed across the yard as Blaine approached. He could hear his dad hitting something with a hammer and cursing. His legs stuck out from underneath a 1932 3 window coupe.

"Is that you, Blaine?"

"Yes, sir, it is."

"Can you grab me that long standard screwdriver? The big one?"

Blaine dug around in the toolbox and grabbed the screwdriver. "Here you go." He handed the screwdriver to the outstretched hand from under the car.

"What are you doing, dad?"

"Well, Blaine, I am trying to fix this u-joint on the 3rd member."

"Can I help?"

"Nah, I am already finished. But, thank you."

"You want to have a beer?"

"Um, sure."

Blaine grabbed two beers and opened them. Blaine handed one to his dad as he crawled out from under the car and stood up.

They both sat down in folding chairs and watched the sunset out of the big roll-up doors at the back of the shop over the parking pad of concrete. There was a big 40-foot motorhome, a 62' Corvette, a one-ton crew-cab diesel pickup, a ski-boat, and his dad's Mercedes 500 Kompressor. His mom's car, a brown 1986 Toyota Corolla, and Blaine's 1972 primer gray bug were always parked in the driveway in the front of the house.

Blaine's dad was a well-known corporate lawyer. He did work all over America, but mostly in California. He said he liked Modesto better than San Francisco, and it was a good town to raise a family.

Blaine's mom was not as well-known as his dad, but many people remembered her as one of their favorite teachers. Blaine's mom's name is Mandy. Rick and Mandy Swanson used to entertain people at the house all the time. Then they adopted Blaine because they were lonely. Mandy could not have kids and wanted kids. So, Rick agreed to an adoption. Rick had been doing corporate legal work for the Tribe in Amador and Calaveras counties. Rick was approached by one of the Elders adopt Blaine because of the violent deaths of his parents. The Tribe did not want the boy in the area because they felt it would be too traumatic. So, Rick and Mandy adopted Blaine. It was all very quick and easy. Blaine was 4-years old when he was adopted. Already potty trained, Rick had commented to Mandy. They felt he was young enough to blend in well with little effort. They sent him to a counselor initially, and the boy adapted very quickly. Blaine was a great son and a good young man. He was always helpful and respectful. He was a very quiet child, so Rick and Mandy became very quiet as well. The routine was that after everyone went to bed, they would not talk. They did not want to make Blaine uncomfortable. They never knew that Blaine ached for conversation from them. They never knew that Blaine thought something was wrong with them and often wondered why they did not talk to each other. All the while, it was because they were trying to make Blaine comfortable and happy.

It is kind of sad that the three of them had listened to the counselors about being quiet for Blaine's good. Ironic that all that was needed was conversation. Instead, they would always tell Blaine they loved him and praise him for things but never really carried on any long conversations.

As Rick and Blaine sat quietly drinking their beer, Blaine asked a weird question. "Dad, did you hear about the two homicides this month?"

Rick shook his head no. "I have not heard much news. Been really busy with work and the car."

"Do you believe in evil?"

"Oh, sure, Blaine. Humans can be really evil, son."

"Oh," Blaine sat quietly. The silence awkwardly dragged out. Rick kept waiting for Blaine to say something, and he did not want to pry. What if Blaine wanted to talk about that night in the woods? Rick stayed quiet.

"Well, time for me to go to bed, son. See you tomorrow." Rick got up and closed the big rollup door to the shop. Blaine got up and closed the rollup door on the house side. Rick locked the door as they walked out of the shop and headed to the house.

"See you tomorrow, Dad." Blaine held out his fist for a fist bump. His dad bumped fists with him, and they went their separate ways in the house. Rick went upstairs, and Blaine went into the library. A lone figure of a coyote stood up next to the shop. Crooked-Man watched the house as Blaine stared past him at sunset. Rick had been a great choice for Four-Claws. The boy was special. He was like his uncles, Crooked-man and Two-Coins. He did not know it yet, but he would figure it out. It was almost time for Four-Claws to understand who he was.

Blaine looked in the library and grabbed one of his favorite books, SunTsu's Art of War. Rick had told Blaine to read it to understand how society worked and compete with other humans. Machiavelli's The Prince was on the shelf next to Art of War, and Blaine pulled it out and looked at it. He put it back and walked back to the couch. As Blaine sat down, a book caught his eye. It was a book about The Navaho and Their Tales of Shapeshifters. Blaine got up, took The Art of War back to the bookcase, and put it back. He went to the shelf with the book on Shapeshifters and pulled it out. He opened the book, and a piece of paper fell out.

"To Rick. Thank you for what you are doing. Here is an idea of what you will see. You are not in danger, and we will keep you safe." There was a paw mark next to the writing like a signature.

Blaine had a feeling that he knew who this was from. He had a faint memory of one or two people or what he thought were people. He had a faint memory of what he thought were two dogs, and maybe they were his pets. There was no feeling of fear from memory. He began reading the book. The figure next to the shop smiled, came down on all fours, and slowly loped away.

The night was coming over the house. The moon was overhead, casting a soft glow on the yard and the top of the shop. Blaine could see the reflection of the moon in the pool. Sleep was creeping up on Blaine, and his eyes felt heavy. He nodded off on the leather couch like he had done so many times in the past.

Blaine dreamed of a moon-like object opening and something coming out of it. It was not scary. Blaine did not feel anything but peace when he looked at it. The figure came towards Blaine and touched him on the forehead. "You are ours. You are one of us, Four-Claws." The figure turned and walked back into the moon, but not the moon. Blaine had forgotten the name Four-Claws. It was a stupid nickname his Native family had given him. It was like being spat in the face. The scars on his chest from the bear reminded him of what had happened when he was a small boy. He had tried hard to forget about that time. For some reason, though, this time Blaine felt great pride in the name

Four-Claws. It had an honorable ring to it. Like an anointment or honor. Like a gift that was bestowed on him from a King.

Blaine got up early and fixed everyone breakfast. Rick and Mandy were excited to see breakfast on the table, and Blaine was chatting the morning away. Rick and Mandy sat with their mouths open in disbelief. They answered Blaine whenever they could get a word in edgewise. Something had happened, and something was different.

"Dad, have you ever heard the name, Four-Claws?"

Rick looked puzzled. "Um, no. Did you meet someone by that name?"

Blaine looked at his mom. "Um, nothing rings a bell, honey," Mandy replied, "Why?"

"Oh, I had this dream. Weird, but I woke up happy about it."

Rick and Mandy smiled, they both replied simultaneously, "that is good, Blaine." Rick and Mandy looked at each other surprised by their own responses. They ate breakfast and talked so much during breakfast that Rick and Mandy were late to work. They had always thought that Blaine was on the autism spectrum because he was quiet and socially alone. Rick thought about what the Elder had told him many years ago when Blaine was a boy of about 6. He wondered if that man's name was Four-Claws, and he did not know that Crooked-man and Two-Coins had brought Blaine to Rick.

Nine

The semester was coming to an end. Blaine had a 4.0 GPA, and everyone was happy. He will be graduating in a couple of weeks. Blaine was trying hard to decide what he wanted to do with himself. Rick wanted him to go to university. Mandy said she wished he would be was fine with an AS degree in Social Work. Mandy told him he could work at the county as a social worker until he decided if he wanted to go to get a bachelor's degree.

The last three months had gone on without any more dreams. Blaine felt happier than he had ever felt before. He was talking with his mom and dad like a normal family. His parents were very happy as well. He watched as his parents began talking to each other more and more. Everything was going well. He had an interview at the county for a social worker position on Wednesday next week. All is well.

Blaine received a package in the mail. It had a map, a letter, and some pictures. It was an invitation to a meteor watching party at Hetch-Hetchy Dam! It was supposed to be a moonless night, perfect for watching stars up in the mountains by Yosemite National Park. This was going to be great. It was the weekend after his graduation. Blaine pinned the map and instructions up on his bulletin board and told his mom and dad about it. Everyone was excited about the trip.

Blaine's dad Rick asked if Blaine wanted to take the full-frame digital camera to get some photos. Blaine thought about it but declined. He did not know who would be there, and he did not want anything to happen to it. Rick said that was a reasonable assumption, but the offer was still on the table.

Everyone went off to be late tonight. Blaine laid down intending to get a great-nights-sleep. Blaine had thought about sleeping out by the pool since it was warm out now. Mandy had left the sliding door open and some of the windows open to help clear out the house for a nice spring scent. The trees were in full bloom, and the flower garden was growing like gangbusters. The night was full of fragrance. Blaine closed his eyes and felt like he was falling. Falling as if from an airplane like he was skydiving. His heart raced, and the scars on his chest felt like they were on fire.

In his sleep, he raised his head to look at the figure of a wolf or coyote with glowing eyes. It motioned for him to go with it somewhere. In his dream, Blaine got up and followed it outside. In the pasture behind the shop, there was a large translucent moon-like object softly glowing in the dark. It was transparent, floating, barely touching the ground, with an opening like a door on the bottom edge of a giant moon. He looked up, and the object looked miles above him. The figure led him inside of the moon.

Blaine has tried to wrap his head around what he dreamed about. The coyote figure was a man named Crooked-Man. He had told Blaine that Blaine would not say his real name; it was not a language Blaine knew. He had Blaine sit down in a recliner that became a bed. Blaine felt happy and relaxed. He was not afraid. The man put his hands on either side of Blaine's head. Suddenly, as if a light were turned on in his head, Blaine knew who and what he was. Blaine was Four-Claws, Shapeshifter, Skinwalker, a large lumbering brown grizzly bear. He was special amongst his people, the sky people. They came from the Pleiades star system. They were all over this planet called Earth. Four-Claws was being called to end this evil that Broadknife had allowed to begin. Broadknife and Chaske were banished in the in-between world where Crooked-Man and Two-Coins had kept watch over them. Broadknife and Chaske were trying to break their banishment and come back using Four-Claws power. Four-Claws must be on guard for these two outcasts. Our people live many years in the flesh and in the in-between. Humans call us ghosts, but we are just caught in-between. We are punished. We can only come back if we earn the right to come back. Not all who are banished get the right to return.

Blaine asked if Crooked-Man would get to return. The answer was eventually. Blaine could get up and was led back to his home. The figure told Blaine that the sun would be up soon. Sleep well. Blaine fell asleep beside the pool.

The rooster's crow from the farm next door woke Blaine up. Blaine looked around, astonished to see he was outside by the pool. He tried to figure out how he got outside. He must have gotten up in the middle of the night for some reason. That weird dream must have caused him to get up and go outside.

Blaine got up from the chaise lounge chair and walked to the shop; he then continued to the pasture's edge. In the mud were tracks from a dog and what looked like a bear.

Ten

Blaine figured the dream was caused by the book of Indigenous tales. The Cherokee believed they came from the Pleiades. He had also read about the shapeshifters and the Navaho. All Natives believed in the sky people. The Native people believed in their connection to nature as well. Blaine's mind spun with possibilities. Blaine looked around the pool and found no book. He went into the house and found the book in his room. It should have been in the library where he thought he left it. He opened the book to see if there was a letter inside the book. He found it in between the pages of the Navaho. So that is where he must have gotten the figure's name in the dream. There was something on the back of the letter that Blaine had not noticed before.

"Do not tell Rick and Mandy about last night. I know it is a lot to digest. I will see you again soon in your dreams." Crooked-Man.

Blaine felt hot all over. His hand shook, and he sat down on the edge of the bed. On the nightstand next to his clock, there was a flat rock with a paw print and two silver liberty coins and a leather thong with four bear claws separated by black beads. Blaine was sweating, and he felt sick to his stomach. He went into the bathroom and vomited. He washed his face and brushed his teeth. His parents had left the house an hour earlier without saying anything. Blaine did not know what to do.

He lay back down on his bed and fell asleep. He was exhausted for some reason. He felt sick and lost. This was too much for him to deal with. Everything had been going great. He was so happy and so proud of himself and all his progress. What the hell was happening? Was he losing his mind? He let the darkness of sleep take him into oblivion this time. Blaine did not dream but instead slept deeply.

Evil does not die. Evil is an eternal energy. Good is an eternal energy. These energies are always finding a balance. Nature is balanced. Light and darkness are a balance. As above, so below takes on a new meaning when we think of things this way. Things were out of balance at this place in time. Things will get messy before the balance is achieved. Life is messy. Birth and death and all the emotions concerned with it are messy.

In society, we find many ways to cope with the things that we cannot change. We make up cultural rules, religious rules, and laws and we think that rules will save us. The universe has rules of balance. There is no fairness, no empathy, just cold facts that do not care about your feelings.

Because of these rules, humans wear all kinds of masks. We hide our true selves to fit and be accepted. We even hide from ourselves. We have a different masks for different people or groups of people. The universe sees you as you are, although some people think we must fit in to get in, or that we must fake it to make it. While that may be true to an extent scientifically concerning humans, the universe does not care and will eventually expose you. Humans call these moments Karma. In the universe, it is just fact.

Blaine is a shapeshifter. He is part of a race from another plane of existence. Blaine was not ready to accept these facts. The facts terrified him. The thoughts of these facts stood in opposition to what Blaine believed and thought he knew. Crooked-Man knew these facts and felt sad for Blaine. It was Blaine's path to walk. Sometimes you are the bug, and sometimes you are the windshield.

Eleven

Chaske had been trapped in the mind of Four-Claws. They had been bound in reverse. Blaine was to have been the passenger with Chaske to supply his power to Chaske. Chaske instead had bled out into the wounds of Four-Claws that fateful night. Crooked-Man had interfered and was punished for the interference. The fact remains that Chaske was stuck in Four-Claws. Whenever Four-Claws slept, Chaske was able to slip out in spirit and search for weak spirits to possess. Most were drug addicts or alcoholics. Chaske could take them over and make them do as he wished. Chaske fed off the evil of violence. He had to get strong enough to try to break away from Four-Claws before he fully knew who he was and what his abilities were. The time was short because Crooked-man and Two-coins were still interfering.

As Blaine "Four-Claws" slept deeply, Chaske was out hunting for a weak soul to inhabit. Daylight or night did not matter. A weak spirit is a weak spirit. Chaske tried to find a spirit strong enough to do as he needed. Chaske needed to cause as much emotional grief as possible.

Old man Randy, "cart guy," slept in a heroin-fueled sleep behind the dumpster behind the homeless center. Chaske inhabited Randy to take a "test run" to see what mayhem Chaske could cause. It was like looking through a greasy pair of glasses. Chaske preferred drunks because they were easier to control. Chaske always used the victims for several days before committing any violence. He needed to make the crime as traumatic as possible to feed off the emotional energy that resulted.

Randy stumbled around the building before going into the building. Ivy grew outside the building and covered it with brown dead branches and green new growth. The two-hundred-gallon tote of cooking oil sat by the back door. The front doors had folding security gates across the doors. Chaske tried to figure out how to get some gasoline and super glue. He would have to wait until Randy was soberer before he could go into a store and get the needed super glue. He would have to find a can of gasoline as well.

Chaske stayed in Randy for hours to see how the man would improve as the drugs wore off. Chaske needed to know how much control he would have over the man. He planned on leaving Randy before Four-Claws woke up.

Juan and Aaron pulled into the parking lot of the homeless shelter. They began pulling their landscaping equipment out of the trailer. Chaske steered Randy to a gas can on the corner of the trailer, and he stumbled around the back of the building and poured the gas into the tote of cooking oil.

Chaske made sure Randy put the can back. Aaron saw Randy with the gas can as Randy set it down on the trailer.

"Hey, Cart-guy, go away. Leave our shit alone," Aaron waved his arms and started towards Randy.

Randy backed away, startled. Why was he over here by the trailer? Chaske was abruptly moved to the back of Randy's mind. This man was stronger than Chaske had ever thought. Chaske tried to urge Randy towards the store, and Randy decided to go inside for some food instead. Chaske was stuck here in Randy. It would not matter if Chaske was in Randy or Four-Claws, and it made no difference. Chaske was not yet strong enough to control his destiny. Soon Chaske would come back and take what was rightfully his.

Randy was coming down off his high and wanted something to make him forget it. He walked across the street to buy some Night Train wine. He went to the cooler in the back of the liquor store. He opened a pint bottle and chugged it down. He grabbed another bottle and took it to the counter to buy it. As he walked down the aisle, he saw a bottle of superglue, and he stuffed it in his pocket. Randy did not know why he wanted the superglue; he just stole it without thinking. He paid for the bottle and walked back towards the homeless center.

Randy looked to see if the coast was clear, and then he crawled behind the dumpster, chugged the bottle of wine, and laid down to sleep it off. Chaske waited for nightfall.

Twelve

Blaine awoke at 2:22 in the afternoon. He could not believe how long he had slept. He felt very rested. He jumped in the shower to clean up. When he got out of the shower, he went downstairs to start dinner for his parents. Blaine felt fresh and clean. It was strange, but he felt like something had left him. Like a heavyweight was lifted somehow. He prepared a simple meal of tacos, rice, and refried beans.

Mom and dad came home twenty minutes apart from each other. Dad had an easy day without any court or drama. Blaine set the table. Mom got a glass of ice with a Coke Zero, and dad got a Modelo Especial, as did Blaine. Mom and dad went into the kitchen to make their plates, and Blaine waited patiently to make his last. They all sat down at the table to eat. Blaine mentioned the book he found in the library.

"What book," Rick said.

"The book on Native American tales," Blaine looked at his dad's puzzled face, and there was no glimmer of understanding.

"Many do you remember being given any books when Blaine came to us?" Rick looked at Mandy.

Mandy shook her head, "These tacos are great." She continued eating.

Blaine thought that was strange but no stranger than the dreams he had. Maybe it was sent with him, and no one had ever bothered to look at it.

Rick took a drink of beer, "Is it an interesting book?"

Blaine nodded yes. He kept eating and did not respond. It was like he was back to his silent stage again. Rick just nodded and took the gesture as it was not a conversation that Blaine wanted to have. Rick got up and opened another beer.

"Blaine, you want another beer?" Blaine shook his head no. So, Rick took his beer and went out to the shop, and mom got another taco.

"You want to talk about something, sweetheart?" She sat her plate down and looked at Blaine. Blaine shook his head no. Mandy took that gesture as being back to the old Blaine. Quiet time again. She tried so hard to understand Blaine. She left him alone as he cleaned up the table and the kitchen. When she was finished, she brought her plate into the kitchen. Blaine washed the plates and put everything up. Mandy went up to her room to knit.

Blaine was in the library when Rick came back into the house.

"Blaine, want to have a beer with me?" Rick poked his head into the library room.

"Sure," Blaine put down the book he was reading.

"Is that the book?" Rick reached towards the book.

"No, but you get the beer, and I will go get the book." Blaine practically ran upstairs to get the book from his room.

Rick retrieved two beers, grabbed a couple of coasters, and set them on the large round table in the corner of the library. Blaine came rushing into the room. "This. This is the book." Blaine slid it across the table with the note on the top of the book.

Rick picked up the note, read it, turned it over, and read it. He picked up the book and looked through it. "That is very odd. I have never seen this book or this note. Where did you find it?"

Blaine got up from the table, walked over to the library shelf, and pointed at an empty slot. It was next to a law book. "Right, here." Blaine poked his finger into the space.

Rick got up and walked over to look. "That is strange because I just took a book from that spot for my current client, and it was on contract law." Rick scratched his head.

Blaine was puzzled as well. That means the book had shown up this last week. With all the crazy dreams, he thought they were crazy dreams. Blaine became quiet again, and all his questions dried up.

Rick started to tell Blaine about the adoption. "Blaine, when we were first approached to take you, we had already decided that having a child was not for us." Blaine started to speak, but his dad shushed him. He continued, "My client asked us if we would do this. Your mother and I were not interested at the time. It took two years before we decided to adopt you. It is strange because we had some very odd dreams during that time. It was after one of these dreams that we decided to adopt. You see, your mom and I had the same exact dream on the same night." Rick rubbed his head, "Buckle up because this is going to get strange; in our dream, a coyote or dog or wolf thing came to us told us that we were to take you. It was a great gift, and we would be very blessed. So, I went back to my client and agreed to the adoption. The adoption happened lightning fast. I am an attorney, and I had never seen anything like it."

Rick drank some beer shakily. Recalling the dream and everything influenced him. "So, anyway, this man brought you to us and bingo. Here we all are. Your mom and I were not wealthy like we are now, mind you. We had not bought this house. We were both just starting out. You had been in counseling every week, and we went as well. It was a lot of work. But suddenly, everything we touched began to swell with success. It did not make sense. It was like we fell into a puddle of success or luck or karma. This group of Natives is a strange bunch, no slight intended."

Rick sat quietly, drinking his beer. Blaine spoke up. "So, what do you think of this note and this book."

Rick leaned forward, "I have heard the name Four-Claws, but I had thought the man was talking of someone else and not you. The man had a very strange name, and he was a tall, hunched over man."

Blaine and Rick both said, "Crooked-man," simultaneously.

"I don't mean to sound weird," Rick set his beer down on the table, "Once in a while, I see an animal that sits just out of the light behind the shop. Sometimes I think it stands up. I hear whisperings. It makes me want to come into the house."

Blaine decided to tell his father about the dream, the book, the shapeshifter, the moon thing, and the bear. Blaine reeled the story out fast to make it seem not as surreal as it was. When he was finished telling about the dream, he told about waking up by the pool and the tracks behind the shop.

Rick rubbed his forehead. This was too much crazy shit for him. He could not wrap his mind around it. He did not want to believe any of it. Rick begged Blaine off to bed. They both went upstairs to sleep on the weirdness and enormity of what they had discussed. Both thought about the consequences of this information. Rick was terrified to go to sleep, and Blaine slept like the dead until a new nightmare began halfway through the night.

Blaine was jolted awake inside a nightmare. He could feel the adrenaline surging through his veins. He could feel the heat of the fire on his face, and the bright blaze hurt his eyes. He could hear panicked screaming and yelling and sirens. He felt drunk, and it was like watching a movie through glasses that made you feel drunk.

Thirteen

"Hey, cart-guy, what's up?" The night shift walked in the homeless shelter to relieve the afternoon crew. Randy, "cart-guy," stood looking blearily at the man greeting him.

"Hey," Randy half-heartedly waved at the man and stumbled towards the liquor store.

"You can't come in drunk, cart-guy," the man yelled after Randy. Randy flipped him off and continued down the street to the liquor store, mumbling to himself.

"Damn, do good bastards," Randy mumbled to himself, "I will do as I wish." A truck honked at Randy as he stumbled across the street. Chaske urged him forward. Randy went into the store and bought a pint of cheap whiskey. Randy cracked open the bottle and chugged half of the bottle down. He wretched at the strong whiskey but did not throw it up. His eyes watered down his cheeks. As he walked back towards the homeless center, he tipped the bottle and finished it off. He leaned against the back of the building and sat there by the door to the back of the building and let the warmth of the whiskey take effect. An hour later, you would find the homeless center in the middle of history.

Chaske manipulated Randy to get up. Randy picked up a dirty towel that was hung by the oil tote. Randy dunked it into the oil and gasoline mixture. He placed one end of the towel into the oil tote and placed the other down the side of the tote. Randy reached into his pocket and took out a bottle of superglue and a lighter. Randy put the lighter into his coat pocket. He took the glue and opened the bottle and squeezed some into the lock on the door. Randy stumbled around the building to the front and put glue in the security doors and screens. He oozed glue into the doorknobs and anything else he could. He walked around to the back door, pulled out the lighter, and lit the fuel-soaked towel.

The towel fluttered first, then the flame crawled up the towel, and there was a loud whooshing sound. Then it sounded like a jet engine as the flames burst up through the top of the oil tote. The light oil jumped into flame, and the flames set the back of the building on fire. It all happened so fast. Poor Randy was caught in the first blast of flames and was instantly engulfed in flames himself. He stumbled around burning. Chaske got Randy rolling around so he could put himself out. The flames devoured the back of the building. The top and the back of the building were fully engulfed in flames before the alarms went off. The staff tried to go out the back door to see what was happening. The door seemed frozen. They ran to the front door; it seemed frozen as well. Smoke began filling the building, and people began screaming and running to the doors. The staff was getting squished as they fought with the round doorknobs. Someone grabbed a fire extinguisher and began beating the doorknob with it. Unfortunately, they knocked the doorknob off. They had to try to open the door with a screwdriver.

Meanwhile, people are screaming and pushing. It is taking precious time to open the door. Fire engines could be heard in the distance. The door finally opened. The security screen was frozen as well. The mass of humanity pressed against the security screen, and it broke open. The heroic staff member that unlocked the door was trampled.

Suddenly the ceiling caved in without a noticeable warning. There were still people trapped inside. The fire engines pulled up to the building. It was hell on Earth full of chaos. Randy collapsed, suffering from third-degree burns. There were people caught inside the building. There were multiple deaths, and Chaske celebrated the evil energy as it flowed over the area full of people and victims. Chaske left Randy and found his way back to Blaine. He wanted to feel the anguish from Blaine as he experienced the evil firsthand.

Blaine tossed and turned in the grips of the nightmare. He could feel the pain from the burns of the man. The screams of the victims, the smells of burnt flesh. The screams and anguish of the victims because of burns, smoke inhalation—the terror of those poor people dying in the fire. The firefighters arrived on the scene and flood the building with water. The firefighters scrambled to save as many as they could. The fire blazed, and Randy lay screaming from the pain. His eyes were open wide, watching the blaze glow in the dark.

Suddenly, the nightmare was over. Blaine looked at the clock, and it was Six am. He got up and found his parents in the kitchen drinking coffee. Blaine walked into the kitchen.

Rick whistled softly, "Oh, my, you look like you had a rough night."

"I had a horrible dream about the homeless center catching on fire and people being caught inside," Blaine went to get some coffee.

"Oh, my God, Blaine," his mother took in a quick breath.

"I am okay, mom," Blaine took a drink of coffee.

His mom turned up the television. The scene of the burning building on the news knocked everyone silent. The camera surveyed the scene, and Randy, the cart guy, was over by the dumpster. The paramedics were working on him. "That is the guy that did it!" Blaine ran to the TV to point out Randy. "His name is Randy or cart-guy or something like that. He set the oil tote on fire and glued the doorknobs so they could not open them quickly." Blaine was explaining as he watched the news with his parents.

"That is impossible for you to know that sweetheart," his mother tried to be soothing. Blaine started to argue, but his dad gave him a shhh gesture by putting his finger to his lips and shaking his head. Blaine nodded; his father understood and believed Blaine.

Rick walked by Blaine and whispered for him to follow him outside. "You need to call the police, Blaine. Tell them what you know."

"I have called before. The police ignore my calls and information." Blaine explained about the other dreams and the murders. Rick agreed to be quiet and see what happened. Rick left for work, and Blaine walked back inside.

The news said that it was an electrical fire and dead ivy had not been cleaned off the building that was the supposed source of the fire. There had been four deaths so far and possibly more. Three firefighters had been injured, and one was in critical condition. They still had not had a chance to clear the building.

Blaine's mom jumped up and rushed outside to work because she was late, leaving Blaine at the house. He did not have to be at MJC until later since he was finished, and there were only a few things he had to do for graduation.

Blaine felt drained. What was happening to him? The phone rang and startled him. It was the county with an appointment for an in-person interview. Blaine took the first appointment available this morning at 10 am.

Blaine showered and found a nice outfit for the interview. It was a casual suit he picked out. He looked in the mirror and felt he looked very professional. He decided to leave to be at the appointment a little early.

The drive over was detoured by the fire downtown. Blaine had been so excited that he had forgotten to go in a different direction. It was good that he left early because he ended up being on time. There were news crews all over the downtown area. So, Blaine had to park on the top level of the parking garage. By the time he had gotten to the office where the interview was to take place, Blaine was a little out of breath.

An hour later and Blaine felt very confident that he had the job. They told him they would call during the week. Blaine took the stairs to the upper level and looked over towards the homeless center, and saw it was still putting out clouds of smoke. He could only see the very top of the building.

Blaine started Teddy his VW and headed to MJC a few miles away. The rest of the day was spent filling out paperwork, checking grades, and ordering transcripts.

Fourteen

Rick Swanson had his own practice. He is a very successful man. His office looked like an old colonial two-story white house with seven columns across the large bottom veranda and each side of the house and had a veranda across the top in the front only. It was a sprawling six-thousand-square foot. It had four huge fireplaces. There were beautiful rich dark wood floors with mahogany staircases and rich dark red leather chairs throughout the building. The main room downstairs had a thirty-foot wall lined with a bookshelf that went all the way to the top of the 15-foot ceilings and upstairs had ten-foot ceilings. The windows in the front were big four-foot by eight-foot bay windows. The building was surrounded by a large lush lawn with a white picket fence. A rose garden graced the side of the building. And roses flanked the walkway up to the front veranda. The parking lot was on the left side or east side of the building, and the staff parking lot was in the back of the building. The heating and air conditioning were in the basement. Five other attorneys worked for Rick.

Sandra, the receptionist, called Rick on the intercom and informed him that there was an elderly gentleman here to see him from Calaveras. Rick was puzzled by who it could be. The only people he knew in that area were his casino Tribal members. The CEO never traveled to see Rick, and Rick had always had to go to them. Rick walked down the stairs to go and greet his surprise visitor.

A tall man hunched over the desk by the door. The bottom of the staircase was in the center of the room, and the last few steps were only ten feet away from the back of the room and twelve feet across. The staircase continued over the kitchen in the back of the building. It was a stunning sight when you came in the door. The man was dressed in black. His long black hair and gray hair cascaded down his back over the black western shirt with pearl snaps. He had black denim jeans and cowboy boots on and looked like a cowboy movie star. The man held his hands behind his back. His eyes looked like they were black.

Rick held out his hand to the man. "Hello, I am Rick Swanson. Can I help you?"

"Let us go upstairs. I am here to help you." The man did not shake Rick's hand. Instead, he walked past Rick and started up the stairs. He turned and looked at Rick standing there with his mouth wide open. "Are you coming?"

"Um. Yes, I am sorry. You caught me off guard, and that does not happen often. Do I know you?" Rick had walked over the base of the stairs and looked up at the man.

"I am the one that arranged for you to pick up your son. I wrote the note in the book. I am the one you see outside from time to time." He winked at Rick. Rick felt flushed from embarrassment. He felt vulnerable, and he didn't like that at all. Rick climbed the stairs, passed the man, and led him to his office. Rick's office was the biggest in the building. It had a sitting room and two bathrooms. A fireplace was situated at the back of the office. Rick's desk was on the right side of the room in the center of the wall. There were two large leather sofas and two large chairs around a large coffee table. There was a large table that looked like a dining table in between. Two chairs were facing the desk and a large armchair behind the desk. A bar opposite the fireplace on the same wall as the double doors that led into the room.

"Would you like something to drink?" Rick pointed to the bar.

"A water would be fine." The man sat down in one of the armchairs by the coffee table. Rick brought the water and sat down on the couch on the man's left.

"Can you sit on my right-hand side, please?" Rick mechanically got up and moved to the other couch. "What I am going to tell you is going to be shocking and unbelievable. I have been watching you for years. I am Four-Claw's protector. You have noticed me off in the distance." Rick nodded, and the man continued, "Blaine told you of our meeting, the book, and the note." Rick again nodded, and the man continued, "so far, so good. What Four-Claws told you was not a dream. I am a shapeshifter, and so is Blaine. Our people are from what is known as the Pleiades. We are known as mound builders, builders of pyramids, Atlantis, and others." Rick started to say something, and the man held his finger to his lips. "You may want a drink. Blaine has the spirit of his older brother Chaske in him. He is what you would call possessed. The murders that have been taking place that Blaine told you he dreamed of were caused by his brother. This battle is not over. We are in a fight for Four-Claw's soul." Rick got up, walked shakily to the bar, and poured a half glass of Scotch neat. He walked back over and sat down heavily.

"How did I get involved in this." Rick sighed and took a long drink.

"Do you remember the DNA thing you did to find your ancestors? Do you remember you were part of the Haplogroup X in your DNA? The company told you that only a few small groups had that DNA set. The Cherokee ancestors you have passed that down to you, which was why you were chosen. You are from our people long ago. There is something within you that you do not know."

Rick asked, "How do I know this is true?"

"Your heart knows," the man stood up, and Rick's head seemed to swim as he looked at what used to be a man who was now a coyote standing on its hind legs. It then changed into a tall glowing man that almost touched the ceiling. Then as quick as that, he was the hunched over man. "You know me as Crooked-man. My brother Two-coins and I are seen in the community walking the roads. We are living in the in-between. You would think of that as us being ghosts."

Rick tilted the drink back and gulped it down. His eyes watered, "what now? What do we do?"

"I will meet you tonight with Four-Claws "Blaine" as you know him. It will be a way for you to understand what is happening. You will understand then." The man got up, let himself out of the office, and walked down the stairs before Rick got up. Rick got to the top of the stairs as the front door had closed, and the man was gone. Sandra looked up at Rick.

"Sandra, cancel any appointments I have. I am going to be leaving early today." Rick went back into his office and sat down. Soon the whiskey made him sleepy, and he fell asleep. Sandra buzzed the intercom to tell Rick she was leaving. Her voice woke him up. He looked at the clock on top of the mantle, and it was five PM.

Rick locked the building as he ended up being the last one to leave. He walked to his car and got in. He started crying. He was surprised as he never cried. But this, and this was too much for him to process.

Rick called Blaine on the way home. He told Blaine what Crooked-Man had told him. He told Blaine not to tell his mom. They would let mom go to bed tonight under the guise that the boys would be working on the hotrod.

Rick drove a block away from the homeless center. It was still smoldering. The news would report that they were still trying to recover people. Eventually, they would find twenty people that died from the fire. Randy, the firefighter, would succumb to his injuries as well. The police still did not know that Randy had set the fire and glued the doors and Blaine would soon set that straight.

Again, Rick cried because of the horrific loss of life connected to his son. It was not his son's fault, but it was connected to him nonetheless, and he knew it would hurt Blaine. Rick thought that he was trying to protect Blaine, and he thought about what Crooked-Man told him. Rick was chosen to be a protector because of his connection by ancestry.

Rick was so overwhelmed. The funny thing was that he had always made fun of and teased those that said they believed in UFOs, extraterrestrials, and ghosts. He broke out in a hysterical laughing fit. He had to pull over because he was laughing so hard. How ironic. He found proof, and the only thing he could do was laugh. No one would ever believe it. Then it hit him like a ton of bricks. That is how they stay hidden. All the stories and information were out there for all to see, ridicule and laugh at. And the whole time, it was all true. Every ancient culture wrote about it. That was firsthand evidence. The way that the ET's stayed hidden was through ridicule. Maybe they had designed humans to be closed-minded like that.

Rick turned off the radio and drove home in silence. Tonight, would be interesting, and maybe he could get some answers. He could not tell if he was excited or terrified.

Rick saw Mandy and Blaine's car in the driveway. Rick drove around to the Parking area behind the shop, opened the rollup door, and parked inside. He went into the bathroom in the shop and washed his face and tried to look natural and relaxed.

Fifteen

Rick walked into the back of the house and greeted Mand and Blaine. Blaine asked him if he wanted a beer, and Rick declined. "What's for dinner?" Spaghetti was the answer.

The table was set, and a large bowl of spaghetti was on the table with a bowl of salad and garlic cheese bread. Glasses with ice were at each place setting, and there were lit candles on the table.

"What's with all this?" Rick asked.

"Relax, dad," Mandy chastised Rick. "Blaine has good news." Rick thought about how he wished he had good news and chuckled. "What is so funny, Rick." He had made Mandy irritated.

"Sorry, sweetheart, I was thinking about work. A funny thing happened today at work. Sorry." Rick lowered his head and sat down at the table.

"Well, mom, dad, I have something to tell you." Blaine was visibly excited. "I got the job at the county!"

The little family broke out in conversation, and congratulations and all the craziness seemed to disappear. They had a great dinner and great conversation. It was like the universe stopped all the nonsense for just a moment and allowed them to have some happiness and peace for just a moment. Rick tried to soak up the moment, and he tried to enjoy Blaine's happiness. The wonderful taste of the food and the ambiance of the evening. Because too soon, it was all going to go to shit. Soon they would be back to trying to fight for their existence from things they could not control. Rick felt like he understood what bipolar people felt. Happy one second and depressed the next with nothing by anxiety in-between.

They let the enjoyment of dinner drag on for a very long time. By the time Blaine and Mandy cleared the table, it was time for Mandy to go upstairs. Rick told her to just go to bed because he and Blaine would work on the hotrod together. Some father and son time. Mandy thought that was a great idea. She went upstairs and went to bed because she was very tired.

Rick pulled Blaine aside and told him excitedly about Crooked-man and the meeting at the office today. He also told him about his Haplogroup X stuff. He was giddy with excitement over the pending meeting. Blaine was not so excited, especially after the nightmare he had. Blaine was terrified.

"What does Four-Claws even mean? Is it because of the scar on my chest? Am I a human being? What the hell is going on?" Blaine looked at Rick with tears running down his face, and the boy was terrified.

"Well, I am terrified as well. But I have a good feeling that we will get some resolution tonight. I am sure of it," Rick patted Blaine on the shoulder as they walked towards the shop.

The two sat in chairs and stared at the stars without speaking for several hours. Blaine looked at Rick, and Rick just shrugged his shoulders and leaned back to wait. The sky was alive with stars and the lights of planes going overhead. For the first time in his life, Rick thought about the stars and other beings. He thought about what that meant concerning religion, politics, and life in general. Suddenly, he felt very small and insignificant. He suddenly felt terrified and out of control. It felt like he was in mortal danger. He broke out in a sweat, and he squeezed Blaine's hand. A creature could be seen weaving its way across the pasture. It rose on its hindlegs. Rick felt like his eyes were playing games with him. The figure walked towards

Rick and Blaine. It beckoned them from their chairs. Blaine squeezed Rick's hand as they both got up. They walked awkwardly hand in hand towards the edge of the pasture just past the concrete parking area behind the shop. Off in the distance, it looked like a heatwave was making the stars look shimmery.

The figure walked towards them chanting something, and Blaine pulled his hand away from Rick. Rick turned to look at Blaine, and he jumped back from the brown grizzly bear that the figure called Four-Claws. The bear looked like it was shimmering in the darkness. Like Rick's eyes and brain were on strike. Rick felt like he was having a stroke.

Rick followed the bear towards the pasture. As Rick reached the grass, the figure held its hand up to stop Rick. "I am not ready for you yet," it turned to walk towards the pasture with the bear. "I will be back for you. Stay where you are." Rick's legs shook violently, and he felt like he would fall or blackout.

The two figures went down on all fours, ambled slowly across the pasture, and disappeared. The shimmering area of the stars seemed to swallow them up. One second, they were there, and the next, they were gone.

Rick stood there for what seemed to be hours. Suddenly there appeared in front of him a tall glowing figure. The figure spoke to Rick in a buzzing swirly kind of voice inside his head, and Rick did not hear it with his ears. The voice was in his mind. The figure turned, and Rick followed it to the pasture.

The grass was tall in the pasture. Rick stumbled and began to fall. Something grabbed his shoulder and kept him from falling. The air seemed to shimmer and wave from black to bright white. Rick looked around and realized he was standing in a bright whitish room. The bear and the coyote were on the far side from Rick. It seemed like a hundred yards away. A table rose out of the floor, and Rick was laid down on the table. He felt weirdly calm. A device was placed on his head, and suddenly like a flash of lightning, Rick understood.

Tears streamed down the side of Rick's face. There was so much he understood and would never be able to say anything that people would believe. The consequences of failure for Four-Claws and Rick were that they would both be stuck in the in-between world if they failed. Rick thought of Mandy and how she would be devastated.

A large figure of a bear loomed over Rick. Rick reached out his hand to his son Blaine, "Four-Claws." I understand, he said in a whisper. The bear nodded at Rick. Rick's mind flooded with conversation from Four-Claws and Crooked-man. Rick wondered if he could now communicate with his mind as well after all this was over. The answer flooded his mind that it was the way they communicated. With Four-Claws and Crooked-man, yes, he could communicate this way, but humans were not able to do this.

Crooked-Man Reached down for Rick's hand to help him up from the table. The table lowered down to the floor. The darkness seemed to come from nowhere. They were standing in the pasture again. It was not so much a ship as it was a portal to another dimension. The in-between world. A place where you existed but did not exist on Earth. It was like changing the frequency on the radio. It was that simple, yet, so complex.

Four-Claws stood up and shimmered into Blaine. The coyote likewise stood up and shimmered into a Crooked-Man. They knew what they had to do. They had to catch Chaske outside of Blaine's mind. They had to trap Chaske in the body and mind of someone else. That person would then be placed in the in-between world permanently. The poor victim would be stuck there as well. It would be a horrific punishment for the victim and for Chaske. An eternal prison that separates one from everyone and everything.

Crooked-Man turned and left the two standing there on that concrete pad and walked into the pasture, falling on all fours and loping away across the pasture in the dark. Blaine and his father Rick went to the chairs and sat down. They fell asleep in their chairs side by side.

Sixteen

Mandy woke up to find Rick was not in bed. She checked Blaine's room and found him not in bed either. She looked downstairs and found nothing there either. Mandy looked outside and saw the lights on in the shop. She walked out to the shop and found the boys asleep in the chairs in the back of the shop, side by side. She wasn't even mad. It warmed her heart to see the two, father and son. It was Saturday morning, and so Mandy went back into the house and fixed breakfast for the boys.

Blaine woke up and looked over at this father. He tapped his hand and woke him up. "Hey, wake up, dad." Blaine stood up and stretched.

Rick woke up. He looked up at Blaine. "We slept out here. Did you sleep out here with me?" Blaine nodded his head at his dad. "What do you think about last night?" Blaine answered him telepathically. Rick replied, "I forgot we could talk without speaking."

"Handy, isn't it? I am going to go make breakfast." Blaine flashed a picture of coffee and eggs and bacon and biscuits and gravy. Rick nodded his head, yes. This was a great way to communicate. The two started towards the house.

As they walked in, they smelled the bacon cooking. They looked at each other and smiled. Blaine could faintly tell what his mom was thinking. Cooked-Man had not told him about that.

"Can you hear her thoughts, dad?" Blaine looked at Rick when he spoke to him still.

"No. Can you?" Rick's eyebrows raised up.

"Yes. I can, but it is a one-way thing. I cannot speak to her. Let me see if I can put thoughts in her head." Blaine tried to convince his mom to get Blaine a glass of milk without asking her.

Mandy waved at the boys as they walked in. She opened the refrigerator, grabbed the milk, and poured a glass. She slid across the counter towards Blaine. "Sorry, I don't drink milk, mom. Is this for dad?"

Mandy looked up blankly at Blaine, "Oh, I am sorry, son, I don't know what I was thinking. Give it to your dad, please."

Blaine turned and smiled at his dad. He held up the glass of milk. Rick was surprised. Blaine told him, "All I did was try to impress on her that I wanted milk by sending a picture of me drinking milk. She knows I don't drink milk."

"Wow. That is crazy. I am going to try it." Rick tried hard. He concentrated for a bit. "Nothing. Damn it. Well, I guess only you can do it." Rick shrugged his shoulders.

Blaine walked into the kitchen and started helping mom set the table. Blaine was listening in on her thoughts. He grabbed things that she was thinking about doing.

Mandy was very happy. Almost stupidly happy, Blaine thought. At least she is happy, Blaine thought. She came humming into the dining area and sat down at the table. Breakfast was enjoyable, and it started the day off perfect.

Blaine did not bring up the fire at the homeless center. But he called and spoke to a detective named Sam Penske. Blaine told him to check the man called Randy or the cart guy. Blaine told him that Randy was the one who set the fire and glued the doors shut. Believe me or don't believe me, but you can check it out. It was most likely on the video cameras of the liquor store that Randy went to and bought a pint of whiskey. Sam was quiet and condescending. "Yeah, we got this, but thanks for wasting my time, buddy." Blaine hung up the phone.

Sam looked at Roger. Sam had the phone on the speaker so Roger could hear. Roger shook his head, "Damn weird ass people in this town, Sam."

Sam thought for a minute, "Let's go check the liquor store. It can't hurt."

"Whatever, I am bored anyway. Maybe we will get lucky, and this cuckoo bird will be right." Roger winked at Sam, "But, you get to drive because it is your idea."

"You sure it is not because you are still half drunk?" Sam pushed Roger's feet off the desk. "Shut up, and let's go."

Roger followed Sam out to the car bitching about Sam's comment. It was true but damn. Why did he have to be so honest about it?

The homeless center was a burned-out wreck of a building with yellow police tape all around it. There were still coroner vans, fire department arson inspectors, and the feds had even sent some FBI agents in to offer their ability.

Sam and Roger went into the store and spoke with the man at the counter. His name was Deep Singh. There were cameras, and he had agreed to let them see the video footage.

"I can tell you what happened," Deep looked casually at the Detectives.

Sam turned to face Deep. "So, tell us what happened."

"Well. Randy, the cart guy, lives behind the dumpster because they won't let high or drunk people in the center. Anyway, Randy comes in and gets a pint of whiskey. He drinks half of it right outside the door almost throws it up. I am yelling at him to get away from here with that. Anyway, he drinks the rest and passes out against the door."

Roger butts into the conversation, "So that is how he gets burned?"

"Be patient, my friend. Anyway, around 8 PM, I see Randy messing around the back door, and then he goes around to the front. Maybe he was trying to get in. They lock up at night. Pretty soon, here he comes back around the back. He grabs a dirty towel from the rack by the door and dunks it into the oil tote and sets it on fire. The thing explodes and burns right up the side of the building. I called and was on the phone to the fire department right away." Deep turns and walks over to the video machine to retrieve the video he recorded on a flash drive. "Here is the video. You can see for yourself." Sam and Randy are stunned. They thank Deep and leave.

Sam and Roger are driving back in the car. "What the fuck," Sam explodes. Roger was still trying to process Sam cursing. "How the hell did that guy that called us to know what happened?"

"Something isn't right, Sam. How the heck did this weird kid know all this?" Roger looked out the window. "There are a bunch of dead people we are dealing with, and now this shit?"

"We are watching the video, and then we will decide if we will call this kid back." Sam looks over to Roger, who nods his approval.

The video ends up showing much more than Deep had seen. The cart guy had stolen a gas can from the landscapers in the morning. He poured the gas into the oil tote, and then he took the can back. The landscaper could be seen shooing the guy away. Cart-guy or Randy then came to the store and could be seen leaving with a bottle of wine. Randy then went back behind the dumpster, where he stayed until almost dark. That is when Randy goes back across the street and can be seen drinking the rest of the whiskey and sitting down by the back door. Everything else looks like Deep had said. So, the weirdo caller, Blaine, had told them the same thing as Deep. No further information. So maybe he had seen the guy cross the street drinking and sit by the tote—no big deal.

Sam excused himself and told Roger that he had to go meet his wife somewhere. Instead, he drove down to the homeless center and looked around to see if he could find a bottle of glue.

The fire department had washed most of the evidence away, putting out the fire. Sam looked around the back and found an empty bottle of superglue. It was in the bushes next to the back door. The doorknob had superglue all over the handle. Sam grabbed one of the investigators and showed him what he had found. He told the investigator what he had seen on the video.

The FBI showed up at the office to talk to Sam and Roger. They agreed that Randy was the one that set the fire. There would be no asking why as the man was dead. At least they had found out who had done the crime.

Sam and Roger tried to decide what to do about the weirdo caller. Maybe a call back to say thank you and to keep him as a kind of last-ditch chance to solve a crime.

Sam returned Blaine's call to tell Blaine what they had found and thank him for the heads up. He also told him that they would keep him in mind whenever they came across something they needed help on. Blaine told them they were welcomed and hung up. It was an awkward call, and Sam had not even wanted to do it. Now it was over, and Sam forgot about it.

Seventeen

The office for social services in Stanislaus county was downtown on 11th street. The office was nice enough, and the people were nice enough. Everyone seemed to be conscientious and wanted to be there. However, most people in the office were very depressed because the fire at the homeless center had claimed one of their counselors. Arnold Baker was the man's name, and he was the type of person that literally would give the coat off his back to help someone. The people in this office had seen him give the coat off his back and the shoes off his feet to a homeless man. Arnie was what everyone wished humanity could be. He was a unicorn of humanity. The man earned 100 thousand plus a year. He lived in a small house in southside Modesto in the same house his family had lived in since the early '50s. The house was situated on the corner of Lassen and Ustick. He even left the house to the church on the corner by his house. The irony that the man devoted his life to helping others would have made him a saint in most countries. However, in Modesto, California, his death did not even make the newspaper. The people that would be affected the most by his death would be the very people that killed him. Blaine's head swam with the irony of the man's life and death.

Arnold had gotten up early the day of the fire. He had gone to a meeting with the county supervisors to discuss renovating the decaying homeless center. Arnold had offered to donate one-hundred thousand of his own money to help with the renovations.

Blaine thought about how Arnie had done so much for the very place that ended up killing him. Blaine found out that Arnie and his wife Jenessa never had children. They had fostered and adopted twenty-seven kids over the years. Those kids had grown up to be productive people around the community. Jenessa had passed last year from a brain aneurism. She was an extremely healthy woman of fifty-one years old. After all the hard work, the compassion, the empathy this man had given to life and his community, his reward was to be trampled to death after opening the stuck doors during the fire and saving over a hundred people. The sadness of the man's life washed over Blaine. Blaine thought about the concept of God and decided that God could not exist if this is how good people were rewarded for all the good things in life.

Even when Arnold was a child, he was traumatized by rape and abuse. That is one reason Arnold said caused him to be like he was about giving. Arnold met his wife at a foster home. Jenessa was an abused child that had been raped her entire life of just ten years old. The repeated rapes as a child left her so physically damaged that she could not have children. Jenessa and Arnold would end up seeing each other over the years in foster homes. Jenessa was a beautiful girl that was targeted for rape even by her foster parents.

Arnold and Jenessa met each other as adults while they were working for the county as social workers. They both had a doctorate's degree in family marriage and counseling and could have had their own practices. They chose to work for the county instead. The impact these two had on the community of Modesto was impossible to calculate.

The doctors had told Arnold that Jenessa had died of an aneurism and that the aneurism was most likely from the abuse she had endured as a child. The cruelty of life never seems to be surprising.

Arnold had come to work at the homeless center after work at the county that day. Arnold would work night shifts every couple of months. He said it was his way to stay in contact with the people he was trying to help. He said it kept him grounded, and it helped him to remember how good he had it in life.

Arnold drove into the parking lot that day in his old 1979 Corolla. He parked by the dumpster and noticed Randy the, cart-guy, sleeping behind the dumpster. Randy's cart was sitting next to the dumpster decorated with hubcaps, can, and other shiny things. Arnold asked Randy if he had anything to eat. Randy said no, as usual, and as usual, Arnold gave Randy a bag with a large lunch bag. Arnold had made sure it had all of Randy's favorite things in it. Arnold has known Randy for the last ten years. Over the years, Arnold had placed Randy in a place to live, gotten him jobs, or placed him in rehabilitation centers. Randy was one of the broken people in society that would never be fixed. Randy did not have a bad traumatic childhood. Randy was raised by wealthy loving parents. Randy had a master's degree in engineering. Randy had turned to drugs and living on the streets when his wife and daughter were killed in an accident. Randy had been the driver, but Randy was not at fault. It was a drunk driver that had t-boned the car on the passenger side, killing his wife and daughter at once. Randy survived physically but died mentally that day. He had turned to drugs and alcohol.

Arnold had tried to help Randy the best way he knew how. The two men would talk for hours sometimes. Arnold and Randy became very close friends over the years. Everyone knew about Randy and Arnold. It was one of the relationships that people would point to as an example of Arnold's big heart. It was also the relationship that caused so much confusion and grief when they found out that Randy had set the fire.

Arnold's funeral drew only forty people to the funeral. Everyone that did not go said that is what Arnold would have wanted. Arnold was a selfless individual that loved life and everyone in it.

The more that Blaine found out about Arnold and Randy caused Blaine to grieve more and more. Crooked-Man had warned Blaine of the plan of Chaske. This depressed behavior is what Crooked-Man had told Blaine to avoid because it only made Chaske stronger.

Chaske had to weaken the spirit of Blaine in order to take over his mind. He needed to make him have a mental breakdown. A breakdown would help Chaske take over the mind Blaine. Time was running out for Chaske because Blaine had been told he was Four-Claws. Blaine was still too weak to be a threat as Four-Claws; however, Blaine was getting stronger. Chaske had to keep him distracted and depressed.

The deaths had been getting closer and closer to the home of Blaine, and no one had noticed. Chaske felt like he was succeeding in his plan. The plan was working, even though Crooked-Man was interfering.

Blaine kept playing right into Chaske's hands, even though Blaine had been warned about those plans. Blaine thought about Arnold, and the more he thought about Arnold, the more he wanted to be like Arnold. Blaine thought of the young man that Blaine saw under the bridge by his house. The young man had built an elaborate shelter under the bridge. Blaine had been noticing the young man building the shelter under the bridge for months since winter began, and now it was almost summer.

Blaine thought about what he could do to help the young man the way Arnold would have done. He would start by leaving a box of food and water and a note with his name and number to call for help.

Eighteen

Chris Billings lived under the bridge on Wellsford road. The local farmers were being cool about it so far. He had a pretty decent shack built of plywood to shield him from the cold. His bedding stayed dry, and the shack was warm. There was enough room to sleep and have his bike inside with him. He had found an old dresser that one of the farmers was throwing out; the drawers were broken, but Chris had found that a certain sized plastic container fit in the place of the drawers. He could put the lids on the plastic containers and even keep things clean that way. He also had a little trailer to pull behind his bike to carry clothes to the laundromat and back. Just because he was homeless did not mean he was filthy. He rode his bike to a local Planet Fitness to take a shower. He paid ten dollars a month for a membership. He had everything he needed, even a job and a free "Obama" phone. He graduated from high school and was enrolled in MJC for the next Fall semester.

Some people have support systems like a family, and some people do not. Chris's father and mother were the only families that Chris knew about. There may be others in America or the world, but not any that Chris knew about. So, when Chris's parents died from a drug overdose last September, Chris was left alone. There was not even a funeral. The school was of no help because Chris was already 18. It took the property owner seven months to evict Chris from the apartment. After the eviction, Chris moved under the bridge. He finished school, and no one knew anything about Chris or his conditions. People do not help fat ugly kids. Maybe if Chris was handsome, slim, and played sports, people would give a shit. But Chris was fat and ugly, and no one ever helped him once.

Chris had just started drinking a little bit to keep warm and help him sleep. It helped with the loneliness if you were too drunk to remember. He didn't do it a lot because he did not want to be like his dad and mom. But a little here and there never hurt anyone.

Being under the bridge was not so bad. Someone had even started leaving a box of food and water. There were some, and there were notes included that said if you need help, call the social services office and ask for Blaine. Chris thought about calling. He thought he would call on Monday. Chris was storing the food and water in his shack when he thought about the cash and decided to go and get a bottle to drink.

Chris rode his bike to the nearby town of Empire to buy a couple of forty-ounce bottles of malt liquor. He walked out of the store with his bottles and opened one and started drinking. He was halfway finished and decided to ride his bike home. He turned onto Wellsford and was almost to the downhill ride to his bridge when a brown Corolla honked at him and caused him to swerve off the should of the road into a ditch of an orchard. The soft dirt of the ditch caused his bike to flip. It broke his half-empty bottle and pissed him off. He knew where the car was. He had seen it parked in front of the house on the left a hundred times. He picked up his full bottle and drank as he rode slowly by the house and stared malevolently at the Corolla in the driveway next to an old VW bug. Chris drunkenly yelled at the car in the driveway, "Fucking asshole!" Chris continued his ride home, drinking as he went. By the time he got the bridge, he was drunk. He climbed into his shack and finished the forty of malt liquor and passed out angry.

Life has many ironic moments that defy logic and belief. Mandy Swanson worked in Empire at the small Elementary school there.

Unbeknownst to Mandy was the fact that the homeless obese bicycle rider was once one of her beloved 6th-grade students. Chris loved Mrs. Swanson because she always brought him snacks and a lunch. She had tried hard to help him and his family. She had even bought Chris clothes and Christmas presents during his 6th-grade year. Chris's birthday was in July, so he was not in her class during his birthday, but she would have bought him a present then too. Chris had never been given true unselfish love before he was put in Mrs. Swanson's class. Chris really had great memories of his 6th-grade teacher. 6th-grade had been a fond memory that kept him going. It was the reason he was going to college right now, even though he was homeless. It was Mrs. Swanson that had taught him that he was worth love and attention. The saddest thing for Chris was when his parents moved out of the area and out of the school district because he would have had Mrs. Swanson the next year as well because she had transferred to the middle school; life is cruel like that.

Mandy had thought of Chris often, and he was one of the deciding factors on her transfer to the middle school. Chris never did show up at the school, and Mandy had thought the worst. She had felt it was her fault that Chris was gone because she had sent child protective services to Chris 's house to check up on the child's living conditions. Chris's parents knew the system well, and they just moved to avoid CPS following up. They moved a lot because of CPS. They had found that the county did not try to follow up if the child had moved.

People talk about our fate in the stars, but few know about truly traumatic lives. Trauma seems to blur the lines on life and the meaning of life. Few traumatized people ever make it beyond the trauma. They keep the trauma hidden. Trying desperately to hide it from themselves and others like it is a badge of shame and guilt. Some learn that trauma can begin to heal to open and be brutally honest with themselves and others. You can pass the energy of that evil of trauma away from you a little at a time by sharing it. Blaine had been able to do some of that with his best friends. All his friends love

Blaine's dark humor. Blaine just thought it was a tool to help him survive. He was not joking when he would tell them things, Blaine was truthful, but his friends thought it was just dark humor. Blaine had no filter. He was brutally honest. Fearfully loyal to the people who accepted him. Chris had never learned how to deal with his trauma. Chris had turned to drink instead because he had held all the pain and trauma inside these years.

As life sometimes goes, Chris lay in his shack under the bridge, passed out and angry at the woman that honked him and caused him to wreck his bicycle on the side of the road. Chris had no idea that the woman he idolized was the same woman that fueled his murderous drunken rage deep into his drunken slumber.

Nineteen

Blaine and his dad were out in the shop working on the hotrod after dinner. They had been doing this for a while now. Blaine had the day off tomorrow, so he and his dad had a few too many beers. Blaine was sleeping peacefully in the chair on the concrete pad behind the shop. Rick got up and shook Blaine's shoulder to wake him up. Blaine was deep asleep, so Rick left him outside on the pad, asleep in the chair. It was a warm night, and Rick figured he would be fine sleeping out here since he slept by the pool all the time.

Mandy was on her way out to get the boys when Rick came walking up to the backdoor. "Where is Blaine?" Mandy looked over Rick's shoulder for Blaine.

Rick shrugged his shoulders and pointed with his thumb over his shoulder. "Passed out in the shop. He will be just fine. It is warm out tonight."

Mandy persisted, and Rick calmed her down and prodded her upstairs. "He is a man, dear. He will be just fine. We just celebrated a bit too hard because his new job is all." Rick wished he could read her mind the way Blaine could.

The bed was already slept in because Mandy had apparently woken up to find that Rick was still outside. She had gotten up to go get him. Mandy climbed back in bed and told Rick to hurry up. She wanted to sleep in tomorrow. Rick walked out of the bathroom and turned off the lights. It was almost midnight. He was in deep beer-fueled sleep five minutes after his head hit the pillow. Mandy was tired as well and was deep asleep as well.

Blaine dreamed of the moon-like object that had landed out in the pasture. It floated like a big balloon. It was like the pasture was the ocean; the moon-like thing was bobbing on its waves. At first, it was a soothing, pleasant, and peaceful dream. Blaine remembered the coyote that had come that night and introduced him to everything. Blaine felt powerful and strong.

The moon-like object floated over the pasture to where Blaine was sitting in his dream. The bottom of the thing began to open, spilling a bright light across the ground. Suddenly, Blaine felt terror. He was paralyzed. He watched as something dark began to drip out of the bottom of the moon. The bright light glistened off the shining black goo that oozed out the bottom of the orb. The black goo was filling the yard and covering the concrete pad where he sat in his dream. It was rising to his ankles. The deeper it rose, the more terrified Blaine felt. This was wrong. He was supposed to be strong and dangerous. He was Four-Claws! He struggled as the black goo seeped up towards his knees and the seat of the chair. He could not move. Something moved in the black goo like it was a shark swimming towards him. Blaine could feel the danger of the hidden creature inside the goo. Something bumped against him, sending shockwaves of fear through his paralyzed body. He tried to scream but found his throat was constricted, and his mouth was dry. The goo continued cold as death up to his chest, up to his shoulders; it crept and slid up to his jaw. Blaine struggled to hold his head about the goo. It crept above his lips up to his nose, suffocating him. He was drowning in black goo. His mouth opened to try to find air and the black cold goo slid down his throat and nose, filling his lungs with pure evil. Blaine's eyes seemed to pop out of their sockets, trying to breathe. He felt himself falling and falling like he had been pushed off a cliff. Then blackness. Nothingness. The sweet peace of death.

Blaine slept out on the chair behind the shop and woke up when the sun crested over the roof of the shop at noon. It was already hot in Modesto, California. Blaine was soaked in sweat by the time he woke up. The bright sun blinded him as he opened his eyes to look around. He must have passed out in the chair last night. His dad left him out here to sleep.

Blaine got up and walked into the house. There was no noise of anyone being up and about. Blaine was made some coffee and turned on the TV to watch the news.

Blaine looked at the time on the TV, and it said 2 pm. Still, no one was up. Blaine felt a little startled. He got up and noticed a strange smell. He got up and walked into the foyer of the house and slipped on something blackish. His hair raised up on end. The front door was open, and the goop trailed out the front door. He was careful as he walked out front, thinking maybe the toilet had flooded, and his dad was fixing it. He walked out the front door and followed the blackish-red goop to the driveway.

The brown Corolla sat next to the VW bug in the driveway. On top of the Corolla was the head of his mother. Bitch was written on the car in what looked like blood. Blaine shook his head. This could not be real. He had to be dreaming. He ran into the house yelling for his mom and dad. He ran up the stairs and did not notice the bloody handprints on the walls and banister of the stairs. He opened his parent's bedroom door.

The room was incomprehensible. It was a carnival of blood and gore. Body parts were strewn about the room—intestines, a hand, a torn torso, and on the nightstand his father's head. Blaine does not remember calling 911. He must have blacked out while he waited to kneel on the carpet of his parents' room.

Blaine was shattered beyond any trauma he had ever experienced. Crooked-Man was supposed to help them and protect them he had promised.

There was a tentative hand on his shoulder. It was the hand of a paramedic. Blaine was taken to the mental health facility and placed into a lockdown 72-hour hold. This was for the police to investigate the murders of Rick and Mandy Swanson.

Twenty

Chris lay passed out in his shack under the bridge. Chaske had fallen upon a wonderful opportunity with Chris right down the road from the house. To top it off, he was angry with Mandy. It was too good to be true. Blaine and his father drinking to Blaine's success guaranteed that Blaine would be out of the picture. It was the perfect opportunity. Chaske seized the moment.

Chaske took over Chris's body easily. He led the boy back to where the brown car ran him off the road. Chaske was able to fan the flames of rage and urge Chris onto the house.

The boy approached the dark sleeping house around 1 am. The front door was locked, so Chris walked around to the back and tried the door. It was unlocked. He looked around the dark house, grabbed a large butcher knife from the kitchen, and went up the stairs. He tried the bedrooms and the left first. There was no one in the bedrooms. He opened the bedroom door and peeked into the room. On the bed were two forms of snoring.

The boy went to what looked like the biggest form and male and stabbed twice in the center of the chest and then deeply drug the knife across the throat.

Chris went quickly to the other side as the woman sat up in bed. She opened her mouth to scream, but something was her in the chest and took her breath away. Then again, something hit her in the chest. She fell back to the bed. She was gasping for breath. The last thing she felt was a stinging sensation across her throat like a pinch.

Chris blacked out from his self-righteous rage. Rich people running me off the road. Who did they think they were? Chaske stoked the rage. He was driving Chris into a blind murderous rage. He hacked and cut, slinging body parts around the room. Yelling and screaming and slipping on the slick blood and falling out of breath. He cut the man's head off and placed it on the nightstand to watch the mayhem and dismemberment of his wife.

When Chris was finished with the woman, he took his head downstairs, unlocked the door, walked outside and threw the knife in the bushes, and placed Mandy's head on the top of the car of the one lady that had shown him more love than any person in his entire life.

Sam and Roger were the detectives investigating the murder. When they found out that it was Blaine's house, the weirdo that had called them, they assumed he did the murder. They just knew that the knife and handprints on the wall would come back to Blaine.

Roger had not seen a murder so gruesome in the 15 years he had been on the police force. Sam agreed that it was one of the worst that they had seen. The entire house smelled of blood and intestines. You could never get over that scent of death. Large amounts of blood had a very specific smell, and it turned your stomach. It was sickly sweet.

The cop cars and ambulances roared over the bridge where Chris lay in his shack fast asleep. The police had no clue that Chris was there or that he had committed murder at the house up the street. Chaske was stuck with Chris for a while. Blaine was out of reach for him. Chaske did not care because he had patience.

Sam and Roger collected all the evidence and pictures they needed. They ended up leaving the house at midnight.

Twenty-one

The prints from the staircase came back too smudged to get anything. The prints from the knife were smudged as well. However, when the bastard put the head on top of the car, they got a great print from where the suspect touched the driver's window.

The print did not come back to Blaine, and there was nothing on record. However, they had not struck out because there had been fresh blood on the knife handle and large drops of blood on the floor on the right-hand side. The suspect had cut their hand. They had collected the blood for a DNA check. They knew the DNA would not be Blaine's, but they at least had a chance of finding who did it. It would just be a matter of time to see if anything came back in the next month or so.

Blaine had ended up staying for over a week. His family is to be buried the following Friday. His father's attorney, Mr. Ulrich Mueller, was the man's name, had arranged everything since Blaine was still in the hospital. Ulrich had followed Rick and Mandy's wishes. Rick and Mandy had prepaid funeral plans already in place. Rick wanted to be cremated, and Mandy wanted to be buried in a hot pink casket that she had picked out. Ulrich had Rick's ashes placed in an Urn that Rick had picked out in the casket with Mandy. Ulrich had met with Blaine and discussed all the arrangements.

Blaine was still suffering from the trauma of his parent's murder. Ulrich was trying to help him through it as best he could. Blaine was to get out of the mental health facility in the next couple of days. The house was not cleaned and fixed yet. The carpet had to be replaced and the bed and all the furniture in the room replaced, and the room had to be repainted. The stairs had to be torn out and the foyer floor torn out because of the bloodstains. Blaine wanted the car to be cleaned and waxed and parked back in front.

The funeral went as well as could be. Since Rick was a veteran, he and his wife Mandy were buried in the Santa Nella National Cemetery. The service was quick, and only very close friends could go. There were no other family members to attend. Blaine had been staying with Ulrich during the time being until the house was fixed, and he felt strong enough to stay there. Ulrich had already arranged for someone to stay there with Blaine.

Sam and Roger had a hell of a time interviewing Blaine. Ulrich was like a Pitbull. He made sure that those two, "assholes" he called them, did not continue with their horrific treatment of Blaine. All information was to go through Ulrich and his partner Alarik. Alarik and Ulrich had served with Rick in the Army. They had served in Bosnia and Kosovo together. Alarik was a mountain of a man that looked like he could tear your head off and crap down your neck. He was a no-nonsense man that said what he meant and meant what he said, according to Ulrich. The Sam and Roger issue as much went away.

Chaske is stuck in the body and mind of Chris. Blaine had been nowhere to be found. Chaske was vulnerable in Chris's body. Because if Chris died then, Chaske would be lost in the in-between world as an outcast. It would be a fate worse than death because he would never be able to be reincarnated.

Chris awoke to the sound of a coyote howling by the creek. It sounded close to the bridge. Chris opened the shack door and looked out into the pitch blackness. There were no streetlights out here, and with no moon, the was so black you could not see your hand in front of your face. Chris heard someone singing or was that chanting. He heard another coyote in the opposite direction howling. "They must be mating," Chris thought. He closed the door and settled back to sleep. Chris thought about how his clothes had ended up by the river covered in blood. He had cut his hand deeply, and he did not know-how. When he went to the gym to take a shower, he found a newspaper with an article about the murder of Rick and Mandy Swanson. Mandy had been a beloved teacher in Empire for many years. She was well past retirement but had stayed in teaching because she loved it so much. Chris broke down sobbing. Had he done this? Was this his favorite teacher? The only one who had ever been pleasant and caring and loving to Chris? The address was correct, and the picture of her car was the car that honked at him when he ran off the road.

"Oh, My God. What have I done?" Chris broke down in tears. He sat on the bench crying. Someone sent in a worker from the gym to see if Chris was ok. He nodded yes. He left to go back to the bridge. He rode by the house, and there was no one there. He kept riding his bike towards his shack. Chaske tried to feel out to see if he sensed anyone nearby. There was nothing. Chaske was stuck in the brain of this meat puppet. The road takes a very steep downhill run towards the bridge. Chris liked to freewheel the rest of the way to where he went off the side of the road where the bridge started. As he created the hill and started downward, a coyote ran out in front of him.

"Oh, shit," Chris swerved out into the road to miss the coyote. A truck came over the rise of the hill and could not avoid the bicycle in the middle of the road. The impact threw Chris over the top of the truck and up into the air approximately twenty feet into a walnut tree in the nearby orchard that was fifty feet down the side of the elevated road from the truck. The farmer driving the truck ran over to the guard rail and climbed down the embankment to the orchard where the body lay. The body was snorting bright red bubbles out of the nostrils, and the torso was twisted in a horrific way. The legs and arms were clearly broken bent at odd angles. The farmer ran back up to the truck and called an ambulance.

By the time the ambulance arrived, there was a large dark red puddle in the dirt around the body. The bright red bubbles had stopped. The pink foam that lined the lips of the body did not move anymore. The victim was clearly dead. He had lived for a while from the evidence. They covered the body with a yellow plastic sheet. The attending sheriff noticed the shack under the bridge. The farmer had said that he thought the kid lived under the bridge.

The bloody clothes were found stuffed against the pylon of the bridge by the water. Forensics ran tests on the clothes and the accident victim, and they took fingerprints. Two weeks later, the results affirmed that Chris was the murderer. The only information that they found was that Chris had been Mandy's student in 6th-grade. Nothing was mentioned of Mandy's kindness or the love that Chris had felt towards her. All that was left was a news article talking about the senseless brutality of a homeless man that murdered an elderly schoolteacher and her husband.

Blaine remembered the child. Crooked-Man had come to tell Blaine how they resolved the problem of Chaske. He was gone now to the in-between world with no way out. He was isolated alone forever. Not alive and not dead. Blaine said he needed time to recover from all the traumas.

Blaine took a sabbatical from work. He slowly, with the help of Ulrich and Alarik, got back to living at the house. Ulrich came over once a month to work on the car with Blaine. They did not do much. They mostly drank a couple of beers. Alarik had been staying in the house with Blaine for the last month to help Blaine out because Blaine hated being alone.

Crooked-Man would show up from time to time to check on Blaine. It was time for Blaine to be Four-Claws. It was time for him to take his place as a protector. Crooked-Man slowly taught Blaine how to use his gifts to help others. He taught him how to shapeshift, read minds, communicate telepathically, but more importantly, how to protect himself from being harmed by humans. Blaine practiced shapeshifting with Crooked-Man. The two went roaming the area looking to help others. Blaine found out that there were other shapes that he could shapeshift. He was becoming a true Skinwalker. Blaine could now take over a person's appearance or likeness. He could even possess them.

He felt it was time to show Sam and Roger how to help them. Blaine could use his gift to help manipulate their minds into accepting him. They could do so much good together if they would just let him. Blaine could manipulate them into trusting him.

Blaine called the police department and asked to talk to either Sam or Roger. After an awkward conversation, the two detectives agreed to meet with Blaine at the police station.

Blaine drove Teddy, his VW, to the police station. Roger was waiting out in front of the police station. He shook Blaine's hand. Like a flash, Blaine could see how to get to Roger. Blaine followed Roger into the conference room, where Sam sat drinking coffee. Blaine walked in and sat down. Sam didn't even get up. Blaine reached across the table to shake his hand. Sam reluctantly shook hands then leaned back in his chair, reading a paper. Blaine thought Sam was an arrogant prick, and Roger was not much better.

Blaine did not get any vibe that he could use from Sam. It seems that Sam is a balanced man and a wealthy man with no worries, Blaine thought.

Roger, on the other hand, Roger was a mess; he was severely depressed because of the death of his wife. Blaine knew he could use that to his advantage. They discussed the case of his parents and the results of the prints, DNA, and other evidence. They discussed Chris. They lastly apologized to Blaine for being so rude and close-minded towards him.

Sam got up and left the room without a goodbye. Roger stayed and talked to Blaine. Blaine told Roger that he was sorry about his wife, and Roger reacted as someone had punched him.

"What would you do if you could find the person that killed your wife," Blaine looked at Roger. He could hear the swarming thoughts in Roger's mind.

"I do not know," Roger looked at the table.

Blaine said, "You would kill him. That is what you are thinking." Roger nodded his head yes. "I do not think you would. I think you would make sure he went to prison, and before you answer, I can help you with that apprehension."

Roger looked up at Blaine, "Like hell you can; who do you think you are?" Roger shifted to get up.

"I will make you a deal, Roger, to prove what I am telling you. I have a gift of seeing things or something like that. I will send you the information, and you can do as you wish. Kill him or arrest him. I will never tell anyone about it." Blaine leaned back in his seat.

"What do you want? What is in it for you?" Roger leaned over the table.

"I want to help people like me that have been traumatized. I want people to pay for hurting others, and that is all I want." Blaine stood up before Roger could. Blaine walked to the door. "I will call and ask for you and tell you what you need to know."

"When might that be? Never?" Roger followed Blaine to the door.

"Talk to you soon," Blaine walked down the hall and out of the building without looking back at Roger, who had followed him to the front door of the station.

"Fucking weirdo," Roger mumbled and went back into his office.

Sam walked over to Roger's desk, "Well, what do you think of him?"

"Fucking weirdo, Sam, a real fruit loop," Roger was angry and not in the mood for conversation. Sam sensed it was not a good time to visit, so he returned to his desk.

Blaine walked out to the car whistling. He had enough information from Roger's thoughts to get started. Roger had suspected someone from a local gang but could not prove it, and Blaine would start there.

Twenty-Two

The man that shot Roger's wife was gray and skinny with thin hair now, and he still lived in the same area, a block away from Roger. Blaine had parked over by Legion Park, and the man was in the front yard drinking a beer. Blaine watched him and reached out with his mind to rummage around in his thoughts. Blaine asked where the gun we used on the lady at the store was. Blaine was shocked to find out that Roger's wife had been raped and then shot. This man shot her, but his partner had raped her. Roger had tried to pin it on this man, but the DNA did not match, so the case was dropped. The gun was still in the man's possession, hidden in the garage, like a trophy. Blaine led the drunken man into the garage and had him put the gun in a shoebox. Blaine had the man write a note and place it in the shoebox as well. It was a statement of who shot her and who raped her.

Blaine watched as the man walked out into the front yard. The suspect opened the picket gate and placed the box on the ground. Then he turned back to the house and went inside. Blaine got out of the car and retrieved the box.

Blaine drove around the block to Roger's house. He sat there in the car and looked at the house. All the lights were on in the house, and Blaine walked up to the door and knocked.

"What the hell do you want," Roger was yelling as he stomped to the door to answer it. He flung the door open. "What?"

"A present for you," Blaine held out the box. "Don't touch anything in the box without gloves." He turned and walked away, got in his car, and left before Roger could regain his composure.

Blaine felt like he did his part, and he felt great. He called his house, and Alarik answered. "Want to go to dinner?" Alarik declined, as usual. So, Blaine went by himself to a local restaurant called the Fruit Yard.

A local country band played on the back patio, and Blaine got a table and ordered a steak dinner. He was very pleased with himself. Tears slipped out of his eyes as he thought of his parents.

Across town, Roger sat looking at the book with gloves on his hands. There was a gun and a note in the box. He read the note again and again. Blaine would not have known about the rape because the police had kept that quiet in order to prove informants correct. Roger felt sick to his stomach. He turned his head and vomited on the floor. His head swam with liquor. He cursed under his breath as he staggered up to go get a towel to clean up the vomit. When he was finished cleaning up, he sat down in his recliner and passed out.

The country band was not bad. The steak was great. Blaine orders some dessert. Lava cake with vanilla ice cream and a cup of coffee. The meal was wonderful, and the dessert reminded him of his father. This was his father's favorite place to eat. The desert was his dad's favorite as well. A person would have expected his father to be overweight because of the way he ate. His dad's metabolism was still very strong even though he was in his late 60's.

The grief of his parents weighed heavy on Blaine. He could not seem to shake it. He felt he should be over it enough to get on with life. Every morning he would cry for an hour. He cried mostly in the shower. He was very private about his grief, and he did not want others to see it or share it. Sometimes it would flood over him, and he would have to find a bathroom to go hide in until the crying stopped. He felt like he was at the mercy of his tears. He wondered when it would subside. He had just started to have a semi-normal relationship with his parents. It had taken years for that to happen.

Blaine reflected on his past and all the trauma. Blaine kept asking himself, why me? He already knew the answer from his college classes. Some of that knowledge helped him muddle his way through. However, books can never prepare you for reality. The hospital had put him on Xanax. The medication made his head cloudy, so he stopped taking it.

It was getting late, and it was time to go home. Blaine paid his bill and left a nice tip. He drove home and parked at the back of the shop because Alarik's black Audi A4 was in the driveway next to his mother's Corolla.

Blaine opened the shop and pulled out a chair and grabbed a beer. Alarik must have seen Blaine drive around the back of the shop, and he came out to investigate.

"Hey. Are you having a rough day, huh? Get me one of those beers, please?" Alarik grabbed a chair while Baine grabbed another beer. He sat down in the chair and kicked his feet out in front of him. "You sit out here a lot," Alarik said; it was not a question.

"Yeah, I guess I do. My dad and I used to sit out here and drink beer." Blaine stared across the dark expanse over the pasture.

"You want I should go? I will go." Alarik started to get up.

"No, stay please," Blaine put his hand on Alarik's large muscular forearm. "You served in the military with my dad, right?"

"Yes, he was a good man. A bit silly back then," Alarik nodded.

"Tell me about him, please. Hold nothing back because I will know." Blaine looked at Alarik.

"Yeah, Ulrich told me about your gift. No hiding from you." Alarik laughed. He began to tell Blaine about his father and all the stupid shit they did when they were younger. They were all officers together in the military. Rick, of course, was a major, Ulrich was a Capitan, and Alarik was Lieutenant. They had served in several conflicts together. They were all military intelligence. Alarik had been the muscle of the bunch but make no mistake that Rick and Ulrich could kick your ass.

"The bastard that killed him had to have killed him in his sleep, fucking shit bird," Alarik was emotional. "I would have killed him barehanded myself if I had known who it was. Getting hit by a truck was too quick." Alarik smacked his hand on his thigh.

"When we were in Kosovo, Ulrich was shot in the back and went down. He couldn't make it to the building I was in for safety. We were under heavy fire, and I could not get out to help him. I thought he was a goner for sure. When out of nowhere, Rick shows up, he runs and makes this front somersault move we had been taught, but I had seen no one ever uses it. Anyway, Rick makes this somersault move and scoops Ulrich on his shoulder and runs like the wind to the building to my left. Rick works his way over to me, and we call in artillery. He saved Ulrich. As they were loading Ulrich on the evac chopper, the medic noticed that Rick had been shot as well. Rick had never said anything. Anyway, they took all three of us. I went because I was tired of being shot at." Alarik laughed like a mad man. "Good times," Alarik wiped his eyes. "He was a good friend to me; your dad was a good man."

It was a long time before anyone spoke again. Blaine asked, "So my father was a good man?"

"One of the best I had the pleasure to meet. Honest, loyal, and he was generous. Few people are," Alarik began talking more and told of lots of war stories and fun bar fights. This was the kind of stuff that people dreamed of hearing about their dads.

The two talked until 1 AM. Alarik jumped up and said he was going to bed. He walked around the shop and was gone. Blaine got up and grabbed another beer. When he turned around, Crooked-Man was sitting in the chair. Blaine came back to his chair and settled down.

"You startled me. I thought a skunk had come into the shop," Blaine waved his hand in front of his face to fan away from the smell.

"It is you that stink Four-Claws. You smell of the white man. Why do you stay here?" Crooked-Man nodded to the dark, and a coyote came trotting up. It sat on its haunches for a minute then stood up.

"Well, you smell like a wet dog," Blaine said, pointing at Two-Coins as he walked up.

"What does a body have to do for a chair around here?" Two-Coins looked around and grabbed a five-gallon bucket instead of a chair. He turned the bucket over, spilling nuts and bolts everywhere, laughing. He sat on the bucket.

"What do you want? You and Two-Coins want something because you both came here." Blaine motioned to them with his beer.

"I want a beer," Two-Coins said. "You are becoming a white man. You are rude to your elders."

Blaine laughed and got him a beer. He hands the beer to Two-Coins, "Now, what do you want."

They both spoke at the same time, "It is time for you to come home."

"You have been gone for too long," Crooked-Man said. "We only let them borrow you for a time, and now it is time to return."

"What happens if I do not want to go back? Do I lose my gifts? Do I turn into a bear forever?" Blaine chuckled.

"Actually, we can arrange for that to happen," Two-Coins narrowed his eyes when he talked to Blaine. "You are of our blood. You are of our flesh. You should not be here among these people."

"But I am, and you put me here. Why didn't you stop Chaske as you said? Did you allow my parents to die? Did you?" Blaine realized that his statement was close to the truth. At the same time, they did not plan it. They did not stop what Chaske was doing either. They had been nearby when it happened. They had watched over him while he was passed out. They could have interrupted what happened. Blaine did not know this information, but he was guessing, and he was close to the truth.

"We did not have anything to do with your parent's death. We made sure you were not harmed!" Crooked-Man said sternly. "We did our job and kept you alive. The things that happened were not our doing or our choice."

"Well, my father trusted you. You let us all down. You betrayed us." Blaine accused Crooked-Man. "How can I go with you? That is no longer my home."

"Very well then, your choice, but maybe some other time. You will grow weary of these people," Two-Coins spoke slowly and softly.

"Well, when that time comes, I will think about it. I have some thinking to do first. I cannot leave now." Blaine got up and walked into the shop and closed the door.

The two men walked to the edge of the concrete. They drop down on all fours and start to trot across the pasture. Just two old mangy coyotes that talked to each other as they trotted.

"He knows Crooked-Man; he told you exactly what you did. He is not sure about it, but he is going to be angry when he knows the truth."

"Yes, he will be furious, and that is why we must take him to see his elder Three-Bears, the one that saved his life. He is the boy's true father. It is time for him to know. Our ways are different than the Natives or the White men. Four-Claws must be brought back. I thought that he would come back to us once his parents were gone out of sorrow and loneliness. I am wrong." Crooked-Man stopped and turned around to look at the house from across the pasture.

Blaine was lying down to go to sleep. As he lay in bed, he could still feel the presence of the two coyotes off in the distance. Blaine knew he would have to go back and take care of business with his people. He had no idea what that even meant. He had no idea of his true lineage. Blaine belonged to the strongest of the shapeshifters, the bear clan, and he had to go back. The coyotes were like messengers, and the bears were the ones giving the orders.

Blaine had already started helping people here, and he liked the feeling of helping and giving back. He did not want to give up what little he had here.

Twenty-Three

Roger called Blaine the next day at 11 AM. "We are running the prints, the ballistics, and checking the DNA of the partner that is on file. I still do not know how but thank you. If this comes out correct, well, I am all ears."

There was an awkward silence, and Blaine let it draw out. Right before Roger was going to hang up, Blaine replied, "I have gifts of insight that others do not have. I can help you solve cases that others cannot. Let me help; that was our deal. Sam does not have to know. You will look like a genius." Blaine could hear him breathing over the phone. He could hear his thoughts as well.

"Ok, but everything is legitimate. I will decide when to tell Sam. If I decide to tell him. End of conversation." Roger was squéezing the phone tight in his hand. This kid rubbed him the wrong way. Something was off. Roger had no idea what it was.

The ballistics and prints were done by the afternoon. The DNA took four weeks. It seemed like the longest four weeks of his life. When Roger had all the evidence, he took it back to the DA that had denied him years ago. The guy had run for a judgeship and lost the election. He was a real piece of work, a true hard ass. He looked at the evidence and told Roger to leave it on his desk, and he would get back to him. Roger grudgingly left the box and went back to the office. Sam was holding the phone when Roger walked into the office.

"For you, sir," Sam held the phone out to Roger.

"Thanks," Roger took the phone and answered, "This is Roger," Roger made a sobbing noise and sat down hard in the chair. "Yes. Thank you, sir. When will that be available? This afternoon? Oh, yes, sir." Roger hung up the phone.

"Roger, you look like you saw a ghost. What's up?" Sam leaned against the desk.

"I finally got the bastard that shot Lexy and his partner that raped her," Roger began to sob and put his face into his hands.

"Holy shit! How in the hell did you do that? You never even told me!" Sam hugged Roger's shoulders. "I am so happy for you. What now?"

"The DA is sending the arrest warrant over this afternoon. Do you think I can go? That would be bad, huh?" Roger looked earnestly at Sam.

"No, buddy, we are both staying here. We do not want anything to go wrong." Sam sat down at his desk, and they waited together for the arrests to happen.

The day seemed to go on forever. Sam and Roger tried working on cases by finishing up the paperwork. Then they went to go get lunch. They figured if they were not there when it all went down that it would play out better. They went downtown and had a chilidog and a coke. They waited for the call to tell them it was over, but the radio stayed silent.

The radio crackled that SWAT was going to the house because the men were barricaded in the house. The suspects were shooting at the SWAT team. It looked like it was going to be a long night.

Sam invited Roger over to the house to wait. They could visit, and Luan could cook or order out. But at least they could all be together for support. As Roger and Sam discussed dinner plans, the radio crackled again. Both suspects were dead, and one officer was wounded. The officer had a through and through bullet through the calf of his leg.

Roger could not believe it was over. He wanted them to go to court and then be given the death penalty. Sam would have told him that was fantasy land thinking because they would have gotten life in prison at best.

"Holy shit, it is over," Roger was crying again.

"You are still coming over tonight for dinner, and that is not a question," Sam called his wife Luan and made plans.

Roger thought about how Blaine solved this case in one day when Roger hadn't been able to do it in ten years. Roger was curious about what this weirdo could do with his gifts. Maybe Roger could make a comeback as one of the best detectives in the valley. Roger was thought to be one of the best before his wife died. Her death put his whole life on hold.

Maybe Roger could have a life again. Maybe he could start all over and find someone to fill the void of his lost wife. Maybe now he could get over it. Maybe, but Roger knew that it was not that easy.

Roger snapped out of his daydream, "Yeah, Sam, I am still coming by for dinner. I was thinking about how this has put me in a holding pattern."

"Hey, Roger, I know. Maybe I will get my old partner back," Sam patted Roger on the back. "Now, dry those tears pussy. There is no crying in baseball." Roger laughed and got up.

The two men left to go back to the station. Hopeful that life would restart for Roger. Questions about how Roger found these connections on his wife's cold case were on the horizon, and Roger did not know what to do.

Twenty-Four

Blaine Woke up to his phone vibrating on the nightstand. He picked it up and looked at the caller ID, and it was Roger, so Blaine let it go to voicemail. It was too early for this, and Blaine still had a week of time off left from work.

Blaine got up and took a shower. He let his mind wander about Crooked-Man. Did Crooked-Man allow Chris to murder his parents? Blaine thought hard about the question, and there was so much he did not understand. Blaine felt sick to his stomach. Is Crooked-Man trying to force Blaine back to the tribe? After all these years of leaving him here and never making any contact? Blaine became angry about his thoughts.

He finished his shower and went to get dressed. Alarik knocked on his bedroom door. "Blaine, you have a visitor." Alarik had such a soft unimposing voice for a mountain of a man.

"Um, be out in a moment," Blaine thought he knew who it was, and it pissed him off. Blaine took fifteen minutes to get dressed, and Blaine quietly walked down the stairs to surprise them. Alarik stood at the bottom of the stairs with a frown on his face.

"I was coming back up to carry you down here," Alarik shook his head, "It is rude to keep guests waiting." Alarik tapped his hand on the railing as he waited, and he did not move.

"I am coming," Blaine was annoyed. "I was looking for this shirt." Blaine tried to give a weak excuse, and Blaine thought that Roger was waiting to see him.

"These people are from the Reservation," Alarik nodded his head toward the library. "I have brought them coffee, and your coffee is on the table by the fireplace." Alarik did not wait for a response. He turned and led Blaine into the library like a butler.

In the library sat a woman and a man. He was a big man with long gray hair braided down his back; he wore a worn Raiders baseball cap, a faded black t-shirt, blue jeans, and work boots. He was bigger than Alarik, and now Blaine understood why Alarik was nervous. The woman is a tall, dark-haired woman with black eyes and an hourglass figure. Blaine was stunned by how beautiful and exotic she looked, and he could not take his eyes from her. She wore a tight-fitting black dress that ended at her ankles. The dress had no sleeves, but it had a collar around the neck. It showed no skin except for the arms. Blaine thought it was the most beautiful dress he had ever seen.

Alarik nudged Blaine to stop him from staring. "Blaine; This is Ana-belle, and this is Three-Bears. I will be in the kitchen if you need anything." Alarik started to leave.

"Alarik, can you stay, please?" Blaine motioned for Alarik to sit by him. Alarik shook his head walked away.

"Blaine; Let me cut to the chase. I have come to ask you to come back to the reservation with us for a while." Blaine opened his mouth to refuse, "Before you speak. Crooked-Man spoke to you. I am sure that he told you that I am your father. Due to circumstances that I do not want to discuss here, you were put into the custody of Broadknife." Three-Bears stood up. Blaine realized how big this man really was. "Our people, our kind, are hard to keep hidden. You were put with Broadknife to help you learn the human's ways and cultures." He walked to the window and looked out, "The events that occurred with you should never have happened. You were spared and sent to what we thought was a haven until the proper time." The man turned and looked at Blaine, "We are not an emotional people. You were raised in this culture by emotional people. I am sorry for your loss. However, it is time for you to come and join us for a time so you can learn our ways." The man sat back down.

"So, I am supposed to just walk away from everything here?" Blaine responded angrily. "I don't know any of you people. I do not know if I do want to know any of you. I don't want any of this." Blaine looked out the window as tears filled his eyes.

The woman got up and walked to Blaine, "I understand that this is a lot to process. I, too, am sorry for your loss. You do not have to spend your time alone here. All of this will be here when you come back. If you choose to come back." She stood next to Blaine with her warm hand on his shoulder. "Come with us for a while, get to know us; you can continue to help the police as you have been. Come, learn about your people. Come and see who you are." She looked down at Blaine. Blaine met her eyes and felt like he was falling into them.

Blaine caved in and agreed to go, but only for a short time. Alarik came walking into the room as someone called him there. "All things have been arranged. I will take care of the house and everything. You do not need to worry. I have taken the liberty of packing your things. You will find a suitcase by the front door."

Just like that, Blaine was on his way back to the reservation. They rode in a blacked-out suburban. There were two men in the suburban, one driving and one in the front passenger seat. They loaded up in the vehicle and drove away.

Alarik called Ulrich to inform him that Blaine had gone with them. They agreed that Alarik would stay at home and take care of things. Alarik would continue to work with Ulrich at the partnership; he would just live here until Blaine came home.

"Ulrich? Have you met these people?" Alarik asked.

"Yes, and they creep me the hell out." Ulrich responded to Alarik, "Rick and I met them when we were taking care of the corporate legal matters for the casinos. You know the rest."

"Yeah, it is like they can get in your head. I felt weird around them, especially the woman." Alarik hung up the phone. His head seemed to clear up as time passed. It was like clouds clearing away after it rains. He felt like he was drunk and starting to get sober.

Crooked-Man hung up the phone with Alarik. Alarik had no clue that he had been speaking to Crooked-Man. No one had any idea that Crooked-Man had possessed Ulrich in order to make all the arrangements for Blaine to go home. Anabelle had mentally hijacked Alarik and Blaine to get what she wanted. Blaine would be safely home before he knew that he had even left home. Crooked-Man had told Blaine that there were other ways to bring him home.

Three-Bears leaned back in the seat and drew a deep breath. Blaine would be hard to train and bring back into the fold. Three-Bears closed his eyes and slept the rest of the way home. Anabelle would keep Blaine occupied. Her beauty helped her with her telepathy. It was easy for her to control males. Blaine was no different because he was like putty in her hands. She soothed him with kind words and told him to take a nap. She would wake him when they arrived. Blaine closed his eyes and had a beautiful dream full of joy and happiness.

Twenty-Five

Roger had stayed at Sam's house sharing memories and eating and drinking until 1 AM. Sam had never thought to ask how Roger had figured out how to solve the case. Everyone had assumed that Roger had been diligent over the years. No one had thought to ask Roger about anything. Roger had supplied a note, a weapon, and a DNA match. The weapon had fingerprints on it, and so did the letter. It was open and closed. It made Roger look like a genius. Roger did not tell anyone how he did it. Instead, he took the credit and basked in the glory that his wife's killer and rapist were now dead. Justice had been served.

Roger opened his eyes and felt like his head was going to explode. He rolled out of bed and stumbled into the bathroom to grab some aspirin. He filled up the dirty glass sitting on the bathroom sink and took the aspirin. He washed his face, wet his hair and combed it, brushed his teeth, and got dressed.

The kitchen was filthy. For the first time in a long time, Roger noticed the condition of the house. He had been living like a pig for years. The house was filthy. He wondered how long he had lived like this and never noticed? He began cleaning up the house. Four hours later, the house looked like a human lived in it. He threw away the liquor bottles and told himself that he was going to stop drinking. Today was a new day and a new Roger.

Roger's house was the filthiest house on the block. The yard was overgrown and full of trash. The fence was falling over, and the house needed to be painted. Roger made some phone calls and contacted some people to come to the house and fix it up. He would get the house painted, fix the fence, get the yard cleaned up, and start over fresh. The neighbors thought that the house had been sold and the new buyer was cleaning up. No one in the neighborhood knew who he was except two neighbors that were in their 70's. He had kept to himself for many years.

Roger worked out in the yard all day until it started to get dark. He thought about Blaine and went inside to call him. Alarik answered and told Roger that Blaine would be out of town for an extended period; Roger hung up the phone.

Roger put the phone down, and it started ringing again; this time, it was Sam, "Hey, Sam."

"Sorry about keeping you out past your bedtime," Sam chuckled. "Want to come over for dinner again. I promise no drinking, hahaha."

Roger thought about it, "Nah, I am dirty from working in the yard. I have been working on this filthy house all day. I woke up this morning and looked around for the first-time years how I let things go. I started fixing and cleaning."

"Damn, Roger. This really made a difference for you, didn't it," Sam sighed, "I am not going to lie, I have been worried about you for years. I have been giving you hints about helping with the fence and shit. Just figured that one day the light would go on in your head."

"Well, the light is on now. I am worn out from cleaning. I cleaned the whole house and started on the yard. Holy shit, I was out to lunch for a long time." There was an awkward silence between them, "Raincheck, Sam?"

"Sure, Roger. Raincheck." Sam hung up the phone.

"Hey, Luan. Guess what Roger has been doing all day?" Luan walked into the room. "Did you hear me, Luan?"

"I didn't hear what you said," she pointed to the laundry room, "I was doing the laundry."

"I said that Roger has been cleaning up his house and yard all day."

"Wow. This case really had him frozen in time. He has been living like a pig for years." She looked at Sam, "If I ever die, Sam, don't do that. Go shoot yourself or something, but don't let the house go to shit."

Sam laughed, "Wow. What a concerned shit head." They both laughed about it. Luan went back to doing laundry, and Sam went back to reading a book about the body farm and the forensics in the book about judging the times of death.

Across town, Roger was fighting his craving to drink. If he was going to make a fresh start in life, he had to stop drinking. This is going to be a hell of a fight, Roger thought. He went to his car and drove to Walmart to try and find something to do as a hobby besides drinking.

The nearby Walmart was open 24-hours a day. It must be the first or the third of the month because everyone and their cousin were at Walmart. It was 9:30 PM. The store was slammed with people. Roger walked in and made a beeline for the McDonalds and bought a cup of coffee and some French fries. He sat down at a table and watched the circus of people go by.

"Hey, this your first time?" An old veteran sat down at the table next to Roger. Before Roger could answer, the veteran continued, "Yeah, when my wife died, I started coming here to watch the crazy people go by to pass the time. I was originally looking for a hobby and stumbled onto doing this." The old veteran laughed.

"Yeah, I came in here looking for a hobby myself." Roger left it at that. He drank his coffee and ate his French fries.

"Well, fella, it gets better after midnight. That is when the freaks come out. It is a good show." The old veteran got up and walked off to go shopping.

Roger stayed until his fries and his coffee were gone. It was an interesting parade of humanity. He walked back to the sporting goods section. On the way, he got distracted in the book section, then electronics, and finally sporting goods. He didn't find anything interesting at all. On his way out of sporting goods, he went through the toy section. He saw a truck model on the cap of the aisle and decided to look at the other models. He had forgotten how much he loved building models. He took a walk into home goods and found an unattended cart and took it with him.

He placed the items in the cart on the display table in the middle of the main aisle. He happily pushed his cart to the models and grabbed four models, some glue, paint, Exacto knives, and an airbrush. These would keep him occupied for a start. He had a lot of happy memories of building car models as a kid.

Roger spotted a clerk in the electronics section and asked if they could check him out. The clerk was hesitant, but Roger told her that he was an officer and he had a call to go to and needed to hurry. She rang up his stuff and stapled a receipt on the bag. The kid checking receipts and bags didn't even look at Roger as he went through. It was like he was committing a crime. He was giddy with excitement.

He stuffed his new hobby into the car. He headed over the bridge by the airport. He could see people down by the river with a fire camping out. There were a lot of homeless people around now. As Roger drove home, he noticed how run down the area was. He had lived here for years and was so out of tune until now. It hit him like a train. He wanted out of the neighborhood.

After work or during work, he would start looking around at houses and whether he would sell or rent his house. It was supposed to be a new start and a new life.

Roger placed his models on the table and spread out all the stuff. He opened a model and started putting it together. Time melted away as he worked for hours on the model. He had the car model ninety percent finished when he looked up at the clock. It was midnight! Roger cleaned up and went to bed.

There are a lot of noises in the airport district: screams, sirens, yelling, shots, screeching brakes, or tire peeling out. Roger had been drunk for so long he had not noticed all the noise. As they say in the hood, when it gets quiet, then something is happening. Most likely, something is being stolen. There were more people walking around at night than in the daytime. Roger tossed and turned and could not sleep. He grabbed his gear bag and found a pair of hearing protectors and used those. These allowed him to sleep. Sleep Roger did, right through his alarm and the ringing phone call from Sam asking where he was. The sun peaked through the window and woke him up. It's 8 AM! He was supposed to be at work at 7 AM. He grabbed a hat and got dressed and ran out of the house. He drove like a mad man to work. He called Sam on his way and told him what had happened.

Sam laughed at Roger and told him to hurry up. Roger hung up; he was a mile away from work. Roger parked in the visitors parking out in front of the station and walked inside nonchalantly. It was 8:20 AM. Sam was pointing to his watch. He walked over to Roger and whispered, "The chief came by, and I told him you were picking something up for a case."

"Thanks, buddy." Roger rummaged through his drawer and found an envelope full of prints and ballistics he picked up yesterday. He had forgotten about them.

"Roger! Where the hell have you been?" The chief is an irritatingly loud and overconfident man. Sam says the chief has little man syndrome because he is 5'6". "What were you picking up, Roger?"

Sam turned and walked into the coffee area. Roger held up the envelope, "Here is the report, chief; we have been waiting for the prints and ballistics of that murder in westside by Martin Luther King." It was true that they were checking leads on the drive-by from the westside, where a preteen died. She wasn't even the target, and she was in her bedroom sleeping—another sad reminder of how dangerous Modesto, California, had become.

The chief grabbed the envelope and looked at the reports. "Hey, did you see where it says the passenger's prints came upon one of the shell casings?"

"I have not had a chance to read them. Remember, I just picked them up." Roger was floored. They could have had the kid brought in for questioning if he had read the report. "I will get an arrest warrant for the passenger."

Sam's ears perked up when Roger mentioned an arrest warrant. "What do we have here? A little bit of fun today?" Sam loved working homicides. He was an addict for the excitement. "Where does he live?"

Roger read the information on the suspect, "It says here that he lives on Robertson Road at the projects."

The chief looks at Roger, "Well, you two can't go out there alone. We will round up SWAT and take three or four squad cars. You two can oversee it this time. Maybe, we will get lucky and have the suspects come in alive this time." The chief chuckles at his cheap shot about Roger's wife's case.

Sam and Roger look at each other and shrug their shoulders. They didn't care because they were not there when it happened. The SWAT team was the ones that loved to get into gun battles. Sam and Roger had fired their weapons one time in the line of duty. Both were on the same day, same time, and same suspect that lived. There were bullet holes everywhere. All three of them were horrible shots. Sam and Roger emptied two magazines each, and the suspect emptied his magazine, and then the gunfight was over. Sam and Roger laugh about it all the time. There was even a hole in the roof of the carport they were hiding. That guy was lucky to be alive because if SWAT had been there? The suspect would have been dead. SWAT does not miss.

Roger and Sam grabbed their gear bags and packed their car. They met with SWAT and the other cruisers and two canines to discuss their plan. The plan was to surround the apartment the suspect was in and then notify the suspect they were there with an arrest warrant. The canine officer asked them to let the guy run a little if he got out of the apartment so his dog could get some practice. The chief radioed that they would have air support as well, just in case.

The projects were towards the end of Robertson Road across from the park and the water treatment plant. It was a notorious area for hating cops. Cops did not go there unless it was in force. They lost one squad car there, and the officer barely made it out alive. The residents destroyed the car and set it on fire. They beat the officer so bad he had to go to the hospital with a brocket jaw, eye socket, and a nasty concussion. The officer quit the force that year over the incident. Now when they go to Robertson Road Projects? The police go deep in the hood, no less than five or six squad cars.

Everyone got in place SWAT was locked, cocked, and ready to rock. The voice on the PA system told the young man to come out with his hands up. The door opened, and the kid came right out. He was shaking in his shoes. That never happens with these criminals. The kid was crying and screaming not to kill him. His mother was screaming and crying, don't kill her baby. Pretty soon, everyone was outside yelling not to kill the poor kid. The kid is on his knees with his hands up, ready to be arrested. SWAT grabs the kid and puts him in the van, and everyone high tails it out of the hood. You cannot stay and let the whole hood get wound up into a frenzy.

The kid gets to the jail, but before we can even question the kid, his mom has an attorney at our office. I think the attorney got to us before the kid even got processed. Roger was sure the kid would end up getting off on some stupid excuse. The DA was not trying to make any waves before the elections. This case was a case that could make or break your career. Election time was not the time to find out.

Twenty-Six

Blaine looked around at the trees in the Eldorado National Forrest. It looked and sounded peaceful. Blaine breathed in the scent of the woods. The pine scent and mountain misery smelled like strong citrus. They had arrived at a cabin deep in the mountains.

"This is our home. I will show you many things. Once you learn these things, you are not to be interfering with human affairs." Three-Bears spoke quietly. Blaine started towards the cabin. "Not there. Follow Ana-Belle." Three- Bears pointed to Anabelle, waiting for Blaine at the edge of the clearing.

Blaine walked to her, and when he got close, she turned and walked into the forest. Blaine followed her quick, quiet steps. She made no noise while she walked. It was like she was floating. Blaine had to run to stay up with her, and she was still pulling away from him.

Blaine put his head down to see his footing, and when he looked up, she was gone. They had come to another clearing that led to a cliff of rock. Blaine searched for her, and he could not find her. He was angry. He had only looked down for a second, and she was gone, but gone where.

He craned his neck up to search the side of the cliff. Anabelle tapped his shoulder. "What are you looking for?"

Blaine yelped out of shock, "Shit. Shit, I was looking for you. Where did you go?"

"Watch and pay attention." Anabelle walked straight into the side of the granite rocks. Everything seemed to shimmer as she did this. Blaine stopped again. He looked around to see what he had missed. Suddenly she was standing in front of him again. "You are slow-witted. Here, hold my hand." She walked straight into the side of the rocks and not the rocks. Blaine's head swam with confusion.

"It is a portal, Blaine," Anabelle spoke softly. She did not move her lips. "This is how we travel long distances. Did you think we ran?"

Blaine stared at her; he began to speak. "Shhh, Blaine. You must learn to use your mind."

Blaine tried as he did with Crooked-Man and his father, "I thought it was a ship of some kind."

"Much to learn, Four-Claws. Much to learn." Anabelle kept walking, and Blaine followed.

"Do you hear everything that others think?" Blaine inquired.

"No. Did you hear us talking on the way home? No, you did not." Anabelle was a matter of fact in the way she spoke.

Blaine followed quietly behind Anabelle as they traveled deep into what Blaine thought was the mountain. Blaine had not noticed that it was not dark inside. There was a soft light so you could see where you were going.

Again, Blaine started with questions, "How does this work?" Information poured into his head. Quantum physics, frequency, string theory, multiple universes, time travel, dimensional shifts, light speed, bending of time and gravity, and all of it was too much for Blaine.

Ana-Belle smirked, "You wanted to know. Now, maybe you will understand when I say that you must take it a little at a time. Humans have not figured this out. They have theories. We have tried to tell them, but they do not understand. Maybe one day they will be able to understand. The humans still confuse their concept of God/Satan/Religion with us."

"Where are we?" Blaine looked at Anabelle.

Again, Anabelle gave him a dump of information, "We are in the same spot but in a different dimension. We can shift in and out of dimensions at will. You can, too, once you learn. That is how Crooked-Man got this reputation among the locals and other humans." Anabelle showed Blaine what Crooked-Man was doing, and it was like learning how a magic trick is done. It took away all the magic.

Blaine asked again, "Can we do this anywhere and back?"

Ana-Belle laughed at Blaine, "Once you learn to control things, you can. You could go to Mars, Washington, DC.; yes, before you ask, Modesto. Surely you do not think Crooked-Man drove to Modesto. And he did not fly a spaceship to Modesto." She laughed hard at the last little bit. Blaine's mind was swimming in questions. "Look in my eyes Blaine," that is the last thing Blaine remembers until morning the next day.

Anabelle walks out of the portal, leaving Blaine on a bed inside. She lowers herself on all fours; she becomes a beautiful female deer. She bounds off into the woods, feeling the world around her as she runs to meet with Three-Bears, Crooked-Man, and Two-Coins on top of the mountain. The time for Three-Bears was ending, and Four-Claws was supposed to take his place. The bear clan had always been in charge, and time was short. Three-Bears would go back to their home star system. Others would come to after Three-Bears went home. It had been a duty of theirs ever since they had helped create humans as a slave race. However, over millions of years, the Pleiadeans had felt obligated to protect and help govern humans when needed. Although, humans were slow-witted angry primates. They had little empathy or compassion for one another. It was slow going to teach them anything. They had superstitions that got in the way of everything. There were multiple gods, multiple religions, and some believed that even though one human was darker than another that they were somehow of a different race of humans. They were all humans of different sizes, colors, genders and could not seem to get along. If they disagreed with one another, then they tried to kill each other. Blaine was not the Four-Claws they needed; he had been tainted by the whites that raised him. This was Three-Bear's experiment. He thought it might make Four-Claws a better leader and emissary for the humans.

Humans thought they were superior to everything on the planet. Humans thought they were more intelligent and better than animals. The sad truth was that animals were a much higher order, could feed themselves, and rarely fought. Animals never took part in wars. The whales and dolphins in the oceans were the most intelligent creatures on Earth.

The life spans of humans had been cut short due to the amount of damage they caused when they had longer life spans. Even then, humans did everything they could to shorten their lifespan. They were not a healthy species at all. They were made as a slave race to serve us, and our leaders felt pity for them.

Anabelle could see the others in the moonlight on the mountain top. The stars wheeled overhead in a spectacular array-like diamonds. They waited for her to start council on their future and duties.

Three-Bears called them to order. "I am leaving next season. Anabelle, you must have Four-Claws ready. If you do not, it will fall upon your shoulders. Crooked-Man and Two-Coins will be leaving with me. We will have Morning-Dove help you, Anabelle, and Morning-Dove's father, Red Wolf. Red has many years left and will walk the roads now. Crooked-Man has earned his reward of going home, so has Two-Coins. Anabelle, you have many years left here. Use them wisely, If you will."

Ana-Belle stood up, "What about the other clans? Will we be getting any help from them?"

Crooked-Man answered, "They are all in the change as are we. They will have growing pains too. You can always call on them, but they may not be able to help."

"Then why are we still here? What keeps us here? Cannot finally leave them alone?" Anabelle stood with her hands at her side, balled up in fists.

"You already know this. What did you tell Four-Claws? Did you tell him he was being slow-witted?" Three-Bears looked at her. "The elders have decided. If they see fit to send help, they will send help." Three-Bears washed his hands in the air and held them palm up empty. He turned and walked away. Anabelle insulted Three-Bears; he intended the comment for Anabelle and her slow-witted understanding.

Twenty-Seven

Roger called Blaine, "Hello. Is Blaine there?"

Alarik answered in a very clipped manner, "Blaine is gone on an extended trip to the reservation, and I do not know when he will be back, and I will leave him a message that you called." Alarik hung up the phone, and he did not try to have a conversation. Alarik did not like Roger and his partner Sam, and he did not hide his disdain for them.

It had been months now that Blaine had been gone. Alarik had heard nothing from Blaine, and neither had Ulrich. Ulrich had contacted the people he knew at the reservation, and they told him it would be a bit longer. They told him to have patience.

Roger had been trying to contact Blaine since he had left. Roger called at least once a week. Alarik had been getting ruder and ruder.

Anabelle was trying to teach Blaine the things he needed to know, and she had to start at the beginning on everything. Anabelle even took Blaine off Earth to prove what he was learning. He was getting better at shapeshifting, but he had a long way to go. Blaine struggled with the essential things, like telepathy and using the portal. Anabelle went to Three-Bears many times to complain that Blaine "Four-Claws" was not learning. Anabelle told Three-Bears that she tried to flood his mind with the information, but Blaine's mind was too unfocused to learn that way. The knowledge did not stick with him.

Three-Bears took over training Blaine. This time Three-Bears would use a technique that required both to stay connected for several days without disturbance. The risk was that Blaine would have access to memories and plans that Three-Bears kept to himself. Everything that Three-Bears had experienced and learned in the last four hundred years here on Earth would be exposed. Three-Bears felt that Blaine could not become Four-Claws until he was willing to risk everything. There would be things that would be exposed that would upset Blaine. These events were what worried Three-Bears.

Three-Bears hid the most damning information for a very long time as Blaine began to make his full transition into Four-Claws. Three-Bears did not tell Blaine that it would be irreversible. It would be like a caterpillar turning into a butterfly. You will never be able to back. Their people's history and the mission had to be carried on. The sky people were the watchers and the protectors of Earth.

Three-Bears had lived thousands of years. He had been here on Earth for the last four hundred years. Some leaders were here for twenty-five thousand years. Those long years of watching no longer happened. It was always shorter time periods now. Instead of bringing another here to Earth to take his place, he was going to try to groom Four-Claws to take over.

Blaine finally made his transition to Four-Claws. Three-Bears allowed Four-Claws to see all. Four-Claws was upset that his adoptive human parents were pawns in the effort to trap Chaske. His parents were killed for nothing in Four-Claws thoughts. However, the bigger picture began to take shape.

"I have a question," Four-Claws faced Three-Bears. "Can I still help the humans that I met?"

"Humans are supposed to be left alone. We let them carry on their day-to-day lives without interference." Three-Bears quietly answered.

"Then why are we here? To watch them destroy one another. What are we protecting? Nothing!" Four-Claws demanded.

"You are right. You can help, but you can no longer work among them. Keep your distance from them." Three-Bears walked away.

Anabelle came to see Four-Claws. "It is time for us to find out how well you can shapeshift. Follow me." Anabelle led the way to the portal door. The door opened into a beautiful meadow. Anabelle smoothly came down on all fours and bounded across the meadow. Four-Claws came down awkwardly on all fours and loped after her. They ran through the woods at an easy pace and came to the edge of the reservation where a trailer park with Elders lived. Anabelle stopped. Four-Claws came by her side and sat down.

"These people have been under our care since the beginning. Our people created them. It is our duty to watch over them." She turned and looked at him.

"Then why do we allow them to mistreat one another? If we are protecting them, why do we allow them to pollute themselves with drugs?" Four-Claws was very gruff with his questions.

"You are so much like Three-Bears when he first came here. We are to let them be free." She sighed.

Four-Claws stood up and stretched to his massive height. "It makes no sense. Watchers of what? Protectors of what? Personal freedom? So, what do we do when they war with each other? Watch them die?"

She laughed, "you are overdramatic. We are not here to control them as we did long ago. We created them as slaves to mine minerals and did our dirty work. That time has come and gone. We are instructed, ordered if you will, to let them be up to the point of stopping them from extinction."

"There are lots of gray areas then. I am not willing to watch them destroy each other. You can do that. I will not," he came down on all fours again, "I will try to help where I can. I understand that I cannot interfere physically, but I can give advice, can't I?"

"We will see how you feel about that in time. Three-Bears once thought as you do. He has since changed his mind," she turned and headed back to the meadow to the portal.

Four-Claws followed her as they navigated the woods back to the meadow. Before they walked into the meadow, Anabelle stopped and turned towards Four-Claws, "I have been listening to your thoughts. I will help you. If you decide to stop, I will be there to support that decision. Be clear in knowing that I do not agree with you because of my experiences. However, I will support you." She continued into the meadow and lay down in the grass.

Four-Claws stayed in the woods on the edge of the clearing. He decided that he would have Crooked-man go with him to his home in Modesto. Four-Claws wanted to speak with Alarik and Roger. He wanted to see if he could really help people, or he just wished to help people.

Twenty-Eight

Crooked-Man and Four-Claws came out of the portal in the pasture behind the shop at Four-Claw's home in Modesto. They took on their human form went to the house to talk to Alarik. Alarik was in the kitchen and saw the men walking up. He answered the door with a tinge of excitement. He had missed Blaine.

"HEY! I thought these guys kidnapped you, and I was going to have to come to all Army Ranger style. Good to see you." Alarik shook Blaine's hand and pulled him in for a tight hug. The man was a brute. Blaine thought Alarik was going to break his back; he hugged him so hard. "Hey. Before you say anything, Blaine, call that Roger, asshole. Please. He is driving me nuts." Alarik smiled and waved at Crooked-Man.

"Can I speak now?" Blaine smiled, and Alarik nodded as he let them in the house, "To cut to the chase, I will be in and out. You can live here if you like; Just so I can stay here from time to time. I know it is kind of messed up because you have been here for me, and you put everything on hold." Blaine looked at Alarik.

"Well, Blaine, I do have a home, just saying, but thank you very much. If you need a caretaker here, I can place someone here. They would keep your privacy. I think my niece might be interested. She is a nerd and does not party or anything." Alarik looked at Blaine, who nodded yes. "I will give her a call right now," Alarik called his niece. Alarik is a take-charge type of guy, and after the call, he said it was all finished.

"Just leave me a note telling her and me what you want to be done, and she will do it."

"Thank you. I will need to contact Ulrich and make some arrangements for the rest of my affairs," Blaine looked over at Crooked-Man.

"What? Are you leaving us for good? Selling everything and moving away?" Alarik stood with his arms folded across his chest. "Are you ok? They are not using voodoo shit on you?"

Blaine laughed at that, "No. Nothing as exciting as that. It is just that I have a lot of stuff to process right now." Crooked-Man turned and nodded at Blaine and walked out the door, and he would be back when needed.

"Is he ok?" Alarik pointed with his thumb over his shoulder, and Blaine nodded yes. The two sat down at the dinner table and drank coffee and visited into the night. Blaine begged off to bed at midnight, and they both went to their prospective rooms.

Blaine's room was clean and organized. All the laundry was put away, and the clothes were put in order in his closet. Everything was organized by color and type of clothing. Jeans were with jeans, slacks with slacks, t-shirt with t-shirts, button-ups with buttons ups. Holy shit, Alarik must have been bored. The whole entire house was spotless and organized. Blaine fell asleep as soon as his head hit the pillow. It was nice to be home.

Blaine awoke to the smell of bacon and eggs with coffee. He took a quick shower and hurried downstairs. There in the kitchen were Alarik and Roger. Alarik does not trust Roger, so, Alarik called Roger and told him this morning would be his only chance of speaking to Blaine before he left again. Alarik did not want Blaine by himself with Roger. Alarik had no idea of who Blaine really was. Four-Claws could easily handle Alarik, Ulrich, and Roger at the same time. They did not know that, nor did they need to know that information.

Roger was eager to speak to Blaine alone. However, Alarik was not keen on that happening. Blaine asked Alarik for a little privacy with Roger. Alarik conceded and went into the library.

"I don't think he likes me," Roger whispered.

"That is because he doesn't trust you or like you," Blaine looked towards the library. "It is because of the way you guys treated me in the beginning. Alarik is my father's friend. He is a fierce protector."

"Fair enough," Roger shrugged his shoulders. "We are good now, you and me?"

"Yeah, for now anyway. I came back here to help you," Blaine leaned forward onto the table a little. "I am interested in helping others. I want to make this a better place."

"Okay, I don't know what we are going to make better," Roger scratched his head. "I just arrest people."

"Well, maybe I can help with solving some crimes with you; only you and I need to know unless you want Sam in on it." Blaine knew Roger's mistrust. It would take some time to accept what Blaine could do.

"I will try a couple of things with you," Roger began to tell Blaine about the drive-by he was working. It left a young girl dead; She had been asleep in her bed. "Tell me what you need to do."

"Can I meet the suspect you have in custody right now?" Blaine looked at Roger earnestly. "Just introduce me to him and let me shake their hand. I will be done after that. No need to question."

"Let me see what I can do, but you cannot speak with them," Roger called the county facility and made an appointment to see the suspect. "I will introduce you. You shake his hand, and we are done?"

"Yes. That is all I will need for right now," Blaine held out his hand to Roger, but Roger did not shake it.

"Sorry, but if you can do something with a handshake, I am not shaking hands," Roger shook his head no. "I will drive. I will tell you when we need to go. Okay."

"Sure. No problem. I don't want to drive," Blaine didn't mind being driven around.

It took them thirty minutes to get to the jail facility to see the suspect. Neither spoke on the way there in the car or as they were walking up to the facility. Blaine followed Roger into the interrogation room where the suspect says waiting. Roger introduces Blaine. Blaine shook his hand and sat down by Roger. Blaine wrote him a note. Ask him why his mother was driving that night. Blaine locked eyes with the suspect.

Roger stood up next to the suspect, "Why didn't you tell me your mom was driving?"

The kid hung his head down, "I was afraid she would get in trouble. She didn't know my uncle and brother were going to shoot out the window. "

Roger took a deep breath and looked at Blaine, "Don't worry, it is not your fault or her fault. I will see what I can do to help her." Roger buzzed the officer to come to pick up the suspect. Roger stared at the door a long time, "How do you do that?" He said, staring at the door.

"You wouldn't believe me if I told you. If I showed you the things I could do, you would never contact me again. Suffice it to say that I can read a person's mind. And before you reply, don't forget to call the landscaper back to finish the yard that you started cleaning." Roger spun around and looked at Blaine.

"How the hell did you know that? So, you can just read my mind?" Roger backed up a little.

"Look, I am not some evil thing, Roger. It is not magic, and it is not a trick. I cannot explain it to you any other way. I just want to help people."

The awkward silence lasted for two minutes before Roger responded, "I don't care what you do or how you do it, as long as it gets results."

"Trust me, I won't tell Sam, and you can take the credit for it all," Blaine looked at Roger, who had his mouth wide open. Blaine walked out of the room and out to the car. Roger followed with a confused look on his face. This moment would set up an agreement between Roger and Blaine. Roger would call Blaine, and Blaine would show up and help. This relationship would last for years.

Roger was able to charge the bother and the uncle with murder. He made a deal with the mom and the younger brother. Everyone was happy, and justice was served. Roger ended up getting promoted. After all these years, he finally got promoted. The chief told him that it was a miracle that he solved his wife's case and made such a big improvement because he was getting ready to fire him. Roger thought about how he had suddenly fallen into a lot of good luck lately. Blaine had already helped many people, but mostly Roger.

Blaine/Four-Claws met Crooked-Man a week later behind the shop. Alarik's niece was taking over the house for Blaine. She had a number to contact Blaine if need be. Four-Claws looked back at the house and quietly said his good-byes. He did not know where life would take him now.

The weight of the coming year was pressing on Four-Claws. Three-Bears would be leaving soon. Four-Claws was already assuming his role as a leader. He had lots of support from Anabelle, Crooked-Man, and Two-Coins. Four-Claws had decided it was time to stop watching and start protecting.